Sarah Farley Hills

Holding Hands

Sarah Farley Hills

Holding Hands

First Love

JustFiction Edition

Impressum/Imprint (nur für Deutschland/only for Germany)
Bibliografische Information der Deutschen Nationalbibliothek: Die Deutsche Nationalbibliothek verzeichnet diese Publikation in der Deutschen Nationalbibliografie; detaillierte bibliografische Daten sind im Internet über http://dnb.d-nb.de abrufbar.

Alle in diesem Buch genannten Marken und Produktnamen unterliegen warenzeichen-, marken- oder patentrechtlichem Schutz bzw. sind Warenzeichen oder eingetragene Warenzeichen der jeweiligen Inhaber. Die Wiedergabe von Marken, Produktnamen, Gebrauchsnamen, Handelsnamen, Warenbezeichnungen u.s.w. in diesem Werk berechtigt auch ohne besondere Kennzeichnung nicht zu der Annahme, dass solche Namen im Sinne der Warenzeichen- und Markenschutzgesetzgebung als frei zu betrachten wären und daher von jedermann benutzt werden dürften.

Coverbild: www.ingimage.com

Verlag: JustFiction! Edition ist ein Imprint der
LAP LAMBERT Academic Publishing GmbH & Co. KG
Heinrich-Böcking-Str. 6-8, 66121 Saarbrücken, Deutschland
Telefon +49 681 37 20 310, Telefax +49 681 37 20 310-9
Email: info@justfiction-edition.com

Herstellung in Deutschland:
Schaltungsdienst Lange o.H.G., Berlin
Books on Demand GmbH, Norderstedt
Reha GmbH, Saarbrücken
Amazon Distribution GmbH, Leipzig
ISBN: 978-3-8454-4557-1

Imprint (only for USA, GB)
Bibliographic information published by the Deutsche Nationalbibliothek: The Deutsche Nationalbibliothek lists this publication in the Deutsche Nationalbibliografie; detailed bibliographic data are available in the Internet at http://dnb.d-nb.de.

Any brand names and product names mentioned in this book are subject to trademark, brand or patent protection and are trademarks or registered trademarks of their respective holders. The use of brand names, product names, common names, trade names, product descriptions etc. even without a particular marking in this works is in no way to be construed to mean that such names may be regarded as unrestricted in respect of trademark and brand protection legislation and could thus be used by anyone.

Cover image: www.ingimage.com

Publisher: JustFiction! Edition
is an imprint of the publishing house
LAP LAMBERT Academic Publishing GmbH & Co. KG
Heinrich-Böcking-Str. 6-8, 66121 Saarbrücken, Germany
Phone +49 681 37 20 310, Fax +49 681 37 20 310-9
Email: info@justfiction-edition.com

Printed in the U.S.A.
Printed in the U.K. by (see last page)
ISBN: 978-3-8454-4557-1

Chapter 1

Matt

Face book status – Met a really cool person today!

It is a quiet little town with cute winding streets, antique shops and hunger invoking bakeries; the place Amy had called home for the last 5 years. She had moved back here from London like so many others deciding to escape the fast pace, overcrowding and over excitable city where she had studied as a student. The town she now lived in was much more suited to a relaxed lifestyle, with the winding cobbled roads welcoming you in and the close proximity to the sea made it ideal for her. Hythe is a small seaside town full of charm and it makes anyone feel at home in an instant. This place had seen her through some of the worst and best years of her life and it was the area that held some of her dearest and nearest friends.

Her friend Matt is the sweetest guy you could ever know, he said that Amy was one of the ones that bounced through life. He always saw the best in people, a quality that first attracted the friendship. Well, that's technically not true because when they first met, the reason they became friends was because Matt had tried to hit on Amy. There she was lying in the midday sunshine in the local park, minding her own business. She was reading the latest Harry Potter book, when a guy appeared from nowhere and handed her a piece of paper.
He said "I just wanted you to have this" and then scuttled off far too quickly for Amy to even sit up, let alone call after him. She had gotten a brief glimpse of his face and apart from feeling very surprised, she was bemused as to why a complete stranger would give her a piece of paper and just run off? So naturally curiosity kicked in and Amy opened the piece of paper to find his telephone number scrawled in rather curly and artistic handwriting. Nothing else. She smiled. Well this was a first and although it was odd, she felt special because he had gone to such an effort. It only seemed polite that she should text him and find out…well she wasn't sure what she would find out but the temptation was too much.
She texted a quick message saying "Hi? Thanks for the phone number, what is your name?" She decided this was an appropriate opening message, and perhaps he would explain why he had given it to her and then ran away. She was a little excited by the situation. After all she had only expected a quiet afternoon in the park and certainly not to be hit on, literally out of the blue.

He texted back. "Hi! My name is Matt. I hope you don't mind I just saw you and knew I had to give you my number. How are you?"

So his name was Matt, very nice thought Amy. This seemed normal enough and decided to tell him her name, what was there to lose?

"Hi Matt, no I don't mind. I'm Amy nice to meet you." She sent it back.

He texted back almost immediately. "Cool nice to meet you Amy, shall we meet in person, I could take you for a drink at a café in town if you would like?"

Amy was shocked, he didn't beat about the bush, she was being asked out on a date. It had been such a long time since some one had done that. Well, after hesitating, she decided there wasn't much else to do and replied "Ok, that would be good, are you free this afternoon?"

To which he sent "Yes I am, meet me at the Cinnamon Café on the high street at 1pm?"

And that's how it happened. Amy has dark brown hair that is shoulder length; she wears black rimmed glasses and has a soft slightly rounded face. She is naturally very slim and always wears the same pair of jeans on the weekend. She has had the same pair of jeans for 7 years and just loves them so much she cannot bear to part with them. She is a nurse at the local Hospital. Matt is a very tall guy at 6ft 2 and has mousey brown messy cropped hair. He works as one of the local policemen in Hythe. They met for the first time in Amy's favourite café and she knew from that moment on they would be life long friends. It wasn't one of those awkward silent pause dates where you struggle for conversation and wish you were some where else. Instead they couldn't stop talking, at first Amy had thought he had romantic intentions, but it soon became obvious they would just be great friends. Especially when Matt teased her about the grazes she had on her face from a certain recent roller skating incident.

They were just like two peas in a pod, with the same sense of humour and same interests such as going walking and swimming. It was a fantastic afternoon, Amy had made a new friend and the world felt like a good place.

This was 4 years ago and flash forward to today; early November and they are sat in the same café watching the world go by. It is one of Amy's favourite past times, just to sit and watch other people go about there daily lives. She is a nosey person, forever asking questions and watching how other people live, how they dress, who they are with and where they are going. The café is such a relaxing place to go for tea, the walls covered with colourful abstract paintings and soft sinkable leather sofas to sit in. It is a Saturday, a rare day off for Amy and Matt. As a policeman Matt is very successful at what he does and similarly to Amy, he also moved away from London after finishing his studies. They never met when they were in London, after all it is a big vibrant city and they were at completely different universities that were miles apart. Matt preferred suburban town life in Hythe. They would often spend their days off together, meeting up for tea (Amy dislikes coffee as it tastes bitter) and they would explore the local area on their bikes. Matt took a sip of his hot chocolate and turned to Amy, 'So where are we off to today Miss Lucas?'
'I'm not sure, shall we just choose a direction and see where we end up?' Amy suggested, ever the adventurer and to be honest with no better an idea than this to offer up.

'Good plan, lets head towards the coast and take the seaside route' Matt replied.
'Excellent' she said as she drained the last of her tea and got to her feet.

Chapter 2

Sue

Face book status – Is looking forward to an afternoon of shopping!

It is Saturday and officially the day of rest. John, who is a financial advisor, is spending his valued time off in the usual way, down the local pub with a couple of his friends. His wife Sue knew this would be where he could be found and she would often go off shopping on a Saturday and leave him to it. John would take the dog for a walk more often that not as an excuse and the destination was always the Rose Inn. His local was a friendly pub, just 10 minutes down the road from John and Sue's house. John enjoyed having a few beers with his friends and playing darts or watching the football. The pub is a jolly, warm place with an open fire and a welcoming atmosphere.

Sue, who is a civil servant, can never sit still for more than a few minutes and always has to be doing something, so this is valuable time for her and she loved nothing more than going for a good shop with her close friend Sally. They would often drive to nearby Canterbury where there is a wide choice of clothes shops and they spend most of the day shopping until there feet can take no more. Today the shops were unusually quiet and this was a rare occasion for them both. They sped around the shops and made the most of no queues for the changing rooms and before they knew it, it had been 3 hours. It was time for a refreshment break and so off they went to a small restaurant down one of the winding side streets.

Sally is a close friend to Sue and they tell each other everything, often talking well into the early evening about everything and nothing. Sally works as a head teacher for the local primary school and is a respectable member of the local community. She works long hours and has spent many years working her way up the career ladder. She has a family, married to Ted who is also a teacher and they have two teenage children, Lily aged 15 and Ben aged 12. The two children attend the local secondary school and are typical teenagers starting to find there own way in the world and yearning for their freedom. Sally and Sue often have dinner parties and invite each other and their other halves around for meals. Sue and John have two sons. A son called Michael. And a son called Matt. Michael is 32 and a successful photographer who lives with his girlfriend Emma in a small terraced house in one of the cobbled back roads in Hythe. Matt is in his mid twenties and works as a local policeman for the area. Sue was ever so proud of Matt and would tell anyone and every one of his achievements as a policeman, often over imaginative in her descriptions and elusions of his detective status. She thinks that photography is too arty and not a traditional and stable career to have. As a result there is a bone of contention between her and her son Michael. Sue and Sally spent another hour sipping coffee and talking about their partners, their children and their jobs. They finally made it home from their shopping trip around 6 pm and John was still out when Sue returned home.

Chapter 3

Lily

Face book Status – Alton Towers trip today!

Lily goes to a mixed comprehensive school. The secondary school is set in the countryside with fields and there are tall trees surrounding it. Today the sun is shining and there are only a few clouds in the sky. The school is a beautiful setting. There are netball and tennis courts, a football pitch, trampolines, a dance studio, a rugby pitch and an athletics field. Lily loves going to school with her friends and enjoys playing sports. Her favourite sports are the high jump and trampolining. She is a very active and athletic type. All the children from year 11 are currently waiting outside with impatience for the bus to arrive.

Today Lily is so excited; she has been waiting for the last day of term for ages! The school has organized for them to go on a trip to Alton towers resort and there is a coach to take them all the way there and all her friends are going with her. The girls board the bus, joyous, screeching and laughing merrily. Everyone has brought sweets and magazines for the journey. The boys race for who is going to sit at the back of the bus and bundle each other. Lily notices Tom as he runs to the back of the bus with the others boys. He catches her eye and smiles. The bus sets off and everyone chats noisily and the teacher has to keep saying 'sit down' and 'behave children'. About 3 hours later they arrive at the destination. All the children are looking out of the window eager with anticipation. They are given groups to stick together for the day and a map of the park. Tom and Lily have been put in the same group and Lily smiles at Tom. They are then allowed off on their own for the entire day! Lily has never felt such freedom and twirls around with delight. Her friends decide they have to go on oblivion first and then air. Air was the best ride because Lily felt as if she were a bird and could fly through the air. Theme parks are great for children because they can let off steam and run around and enjoy themselves. The next ride they go on is Rita. This is a very fast ride and it scares Lily because of the g force she screams as it goes around the track. It accelerates really quickly and whirls around the track at lightning speed. After this they stop for some lunch they sit on the grass and Tom gives Lily half of his sandwich because she left hers on the bus.
'I left my sandwich on the bus! How stupid of me' Lily says with a frown and desolate look on her face and slams her hands on the grass either side of her.
'You can share my sandwich?' Tom says and offers it towards her.
'Thanks' Lily smiles back at him.
'So how are you Lily?' Tom asks.
'I'm ok thanks, just can't believe I left my sandwich on the bus! I'm so forgetful.' Lily says with a frustrated tone.
'Don't worry Lily everyone forgets things sometimes.' Tom offers knowing something is the matter.
'I had an argument with my brother this morning.' Lily suddenly admits.

'What happened?' Tom asks.
'He shouted at me and I shouted at him. I think it's because mum and dad were arguing last night and me and Ben heard everything. I think my parents are going to split up.'
Lily has tears in her eyes and they spill out onto her cheeks.
Tom gives her a hug and hands her a tissue.
'It'll be alright Lily, don't you worry.'

Chapter 4

Chloe

Face book status – I'm hanging urgghhh

It is Saturday night and Chloe is sat in her flat bedroom drying her hair and getting ready to go on a night out with her flat mate Rosie. Chloe is a petite girl with dark brown hair. She has very striking features and is naturally a very beautiful girl. She is doing her make up and trying to match her red lipstick to her black and white outfit. She works in Central London and lives in North London near Maida Vale. Chloe works as a Marketing Manager for Snap Media. It is a high power job that involves a lot of hard work and socialising after office hours. Chloe is a very glamorous girl who spends all her spare wages on the latest designer clothes and shoes. She lives her life in the fast lane, both working and partying hard. Her and Rosie are heading out to the Cherry Bar tonight to meet a few other girl friends and hopefully go on to a club later. Rosie pops her head around the door to Chloe's bedroom and offers a poured glass of Rose to her friend.
'Oh thanks Hun' Chloe says and takes the large glass of wine and takes an appreciative sip.
'Your welcome' Rosie replies. 'What time will you be ready to go?' She asks and looks down at her watch.
'Give me 15 minutes and I'll be done, so we can head down to the tube for 7?' Chloe says. 'Stick some music on Rosie?' Chloe adds.
'Sure' replies Rosie and she heads to her room and puts on Guns and Roses rather loudly. The neighbours are going to be happy.

Half an hour later, both the girls are tottering in their high heels down the high street towards the tube station. It is early December and they can see their breath as they breathe out from the exertion of walking in sky high heels. They eventually make it into the warmth of the tube train and head into town. When they arrive at the Cherry Bar their friends Michelle and Rachel are already at the bar and soon a round of shots are poured in celebration and excitement of the night ahead. They stay in the bar until 11, guzzling glasses of vodka and lemonade and cocktails to their hearts content. A few guys have noticed the group of girls and are attempting their best chat up lines. Chloe is having none of it and heads to the toilet to freshen up her make up. The toilets are downstairs and Chloe has to steady herself by holding the banister, is it these high heels or am I a bit drunk Chloe giggles to herself. At 11 they head outside and hail a taxi to take them to the Sun nightclub.

'Hello Mr. Taxi Driver, we would like to go to the Sun nightclub please?' Chloe shouts to the taxi driver as they pile in. 'Can you turn the radio up please?' Rosie asks the driver. And they all sing along to 'It's raining men' as the taxi driver takes them on their merry way.

The Sun nightclub is packed when they finally get in from the freezing cold half hour long queue. The girls all head for the toilets as they are bursting, once again there is a massive queue and they eventually get to relieve themselves from the frequent need to go to toilet. More shots of sambuca are lined up on the bar, this time by a man Rosie has met on the way from the toilet to the bar. He insists on paying for their round of drinks and continues to charm Rosie for the rest of the evening. The club has two dance floors, one raised up at the back of the room and the main one below, with a walk way around it. Hundreds of young twenty-some things are mingling, flirting and dancing like crazy things. The music is a mixture of dance music and pop music, it is a great atmosphere and everyone is having a fantastic time. Rosie ends up snogging the mystery man who bought everyone drinks and Chloe has to wait at the end of the night whilst they exchange numbers and say their parting goodbyes. They eventually return home to the flat after stopping for a kebab on the high street and walking home bare feet because their feet hurt so much. Chloe falls straight into bed too drunk to take off her make up, let alone undress. A good night.

Chapter 5

Sally

Sally is the head teacher of the local primary school. She loves her job and has worked at the same school ever since she graduated from university with a master's degree. She started off her career as the reception teacher and then was promoted to assistant head and finally head teacher. She is soft spoken, understanding and a kind person. She has time for everyone and organises everything from after school play clubs, the PTA, school trips, the schools budget, teachers lesson planning and reports to the board of governors. It is a demanding role and very rewarding.

Her friend's children both attend the school, a girl named Hannah and boy named Stuart and it is a lovely safe environment. The school is an important part of the community and they have summer fairs and school fetes, harvest festivals and the nativity play. This winter the nativity play has been organized and Hannah has been chosen to play the part of an Angel and Stuart is a wise man.

Sally is in charge of the nativity play this year and it is very traditional. She has written the script and there is Mary and Joseph and baby Jesus. There are Angels and Shepherds and the three wise men. Some children are characters such as the animals. Sally has to plan the play carefully and make sure every child has a part.

She sits down to write the script and has a coffee. There are about 30 children and so she works out the main characters, the extras and the music that needs to be played. There needs to be a mixture of traditional songs such as silent night, away in a manger and then a jolly number such as We wish you a Happy Christmas and a Happy New Year.

She plans the order of the play, gives each child an important action or words to say. She works through the night to finish the script and at about 5am she goes to bed.

Chapter 6

Amy

It was only when Amy turned 25 that she decided she wanted to be a nurse. She had made this life decision after going through a few terrible years just out of university working in a demanding finance job in the city. The hours were long and the promotional prospects weren't great so she had decided to cut her losses and return to study to become a nurse. She had studied at King's College in London. Amy is now a trauma nurse and works in the accident and emergency ward of the local hospital in Hythe. The hospital is the only one in the area for 10 miles and so very important to the community it serves. The hospital is situated on a hill just set back from the main town and the seafront. It is a lovely old fashioned building dating back hundreds of years and is painted awash in white to bring it into the 21st century. The slope leading up to the hospital car park is long and winding and perhaps not that practical for people without a car. Amy wondered how many people who chose to walk up to the hospital actually made it to the top in one piece? She consoled herself that most people had cars these days and there was a local bus for the pensioners that went straight to the doorstep so it probably wasn't much of a problem.

The front entrance to the hospital had grand wooden double doors with intricate carvings, a lovely entrance to somewhere so clinical and often so full of bad news and illness. As you walked through the entrance you would find yourself immediately at the beginning of a long corridor with side corridors leading off in all directions. There were signs everywhere and it would be easy to get lost if you didn't know your way around a place like this. Amy began her daily walk half way down the main corridor and then right along another passage all the way until she reached the double doors that led to the side staff entrance into the A&E department. It was 7 am and she was just in time to start her first shift of the week. As she leant on the door it gave way because Lucy was heading in the opposite direction and obviously in quite some hurry. Lucy was another trauma nurse who often worked with Amy but on this occasion had just finished her night shift and was looking rather ready for her bed.

"Oh sorry Amy" Lucy puffed as she almost barged straight into her.

"Hi Lucy, no worries, have you had a busy night? You look exhausted." Amy replied.

"Yeah it really was, strange for a Sunday night but hey at least the time flew by, my bed is beckoning me and so as much as I'd love to stay and chat, I'll see you Wednesday when I'm next in - I think we are together on the Rota?" Lucy said.

"Of course, I'm nearly late anyway, sleep well" Amy called over her shoulder as they both went on their way.

At the beginning of the shift there is always a handover meeting where the nurses from the night shift brief the new day shift about the patients currently on the ward and what has happened and what needs to be done in the shift ahead. It usually lasts about half an hour and it is paramount that Amy concentrates fully to all the details given. The A&E ward has a high turnover of patients and often has new patients queued up to be seen in the waiting room around the clock. Today there are 13 patients on the ward and 15 new people waiting to be seen. The on call doctor has just arrived and that means that morning treatment can begin. After a quick cup of tea and the handover it is all off to work and Amy has been allocated 3 patients to monitor and the responsibility of 2 other bays that will have new patients admitted soon. It looks like a busy shift, the same as always and Amy loved it.

The team is a close knit group of nurses who have worked together for some years now. There is Claire, the sister who is the nurse in charge. She is a strict and stern lady just suited to a position of management. Claire is a no nonsense type who always keeps the ward running smoothly with the least amount of fuss. She has a bob shaped hair cut that finishes off curling under her chin, very neat and precision like. She is always approachable, with an efficient work ethic and Amy was lucky to have such a good boss. Amy has a great deal of respect for Claire, she is brilliant at her job and Amy is in awe of anyone who can manage such a stressful and demanding job alongside having a husband and two children that went to school. Amy felt so young compared to Claire. Amy yearned to meet a nice guy and fall in love. She wanted to start a family but it just seemed so far away at this moment in time because she still lived at home with her parents. Plus she led a very unexciting life with little possibility of meeting a man. She was happy enough for now sharing a three bedroom semi detached house with her parents in Hythe. Her mum and dad were ever accommodating and don't mind one bit that she has moved in and out of home at least four times now. The house has an airy open plan living room that leads onto a newly refurbished kitchen and dining area. Her mum had chosen the usual magnolia natural decoration and kept any furniture neutral brown and green colours. It had a sense of calm and was a good place to come home to after a busy shift on the ward.

Back on the ward, Amy is just taking out Mrs Riley's canula when Julie walks into the same cubicle as her and says "Hi Amy, Claire has asked me to assist you with your patient list, where shall I start?" Julie is another nurse on the ward and always presented herself with a beaming smile. Amy secretly thought she must have had that smile glued on at birth. Julie was always a pleasure to work with and all the patients instantly warmed to her. Amy replies "That's great, can you do the observations for bay 3 it is Mr John Bailey he is in with a fractured left arm and broken ribs. He fell off his ladder while painting some windows. Thanks Julie". And off Julie went to do exactly that.

Mrs Riley piped up "She seems like a happy soul that Julie. Wish my husband would take a leaf out of her book." Mrs Riley seemed to continually whine about her husband and Amy had already listened to the story of how her husband had left her in the lobby of the A and E entrance whilst he went off and parked the car. It was as if the car came before her Mrs Riley had complained. A true testament to married bliss Amy thought. She hoped whenever she was eventually married that she would never complain continually about him the way Mrs Riley did about her husband. Mrs Riley is in the hospital with suspected food poisoning and had just been given the all clear to come off fluids and she was hopefully going to be discharged later on that morning.

"Well I'm sure your husband isn't that bad Mrs Riley and isn't it true that any man puts their car before anything else?" Amy said. This seemed to put a faint smile onto Mrs Riley's sour face and with that Amy moved on to assuring her she'd be back later to do her observations and that the doctor would be doing the rounds at 11am.

As Amy closed the curtain around Mrs Riley's bed she caught a glimpse of the doctor going into the consultation room at the other side of the ward. Well that was good news at least he was running to schedule and there would be no room for complaint from Mrs Riley later Amy thought. Doctor Tom Causley was the A and E registrar, he had qualified 2 years ago and was a close age to that of Amy. Amy liked Tom he was a mature person and she had every confidence working alongside him. He had worked on the ward for 6 months and although 27 and a doctor, he was strangely single and unattached. Even so, Amy didn't fancy him, she thought of him more as a brother. She popped her head around the door. "Hi Tom, how are you today?" she asked.

"Hello Amy. I'm good thank you, cycled into work and feel as fresh as a daisy! How are you?" Tom replied.

"I'm ok thanks can't complain. See you in a bit, much to do!" she said and scuttled off to another of her patients who needed the toilet and assistance was required. This job certainly had its ups and downs. The reason Amy loved it was because no hour was ever the same as the last and she got to spend her time talking with and caring for people.

Jake is the nursing assistant, a tall lanky lad who applied for the job fresh out of school and the ward manager had taken a shine to him and given him the job on the spot. To be fair he was very good at his job and he was never too far away when a helping hand was needed. His job involved giving patients who were in over night bed baths, helping patients to the toilet and giving them their meals. He enjoyed his work and was a very cheery guy always happy to chat with the patients and to reassure family and relatives who rushed in with the news that their loved ones were in accident and emergency. He had a natural talent at reassuring the panicking relative and scooting them away to the relatives' room with a cup of tea within minutes of their arrival.

It is nearing breakfast time, 8am and this meant that patients who had been in over night and that were conscious would need feeding. Ann, the porter, has just arrived with the large metal wheelie trolley containing hot breakfasts, cereal, tea and coffee for the patients. Ann is also responsible for bringing the staff their post and today it seemed there was a big pile as she passed it to Amy and asked her to sign the receipt form. Amy sifted through the piles of envelopes, blood forms and results sheets thinking this would all need to go through into the nurses' station. Ann parked the trolley and she and Jake started to hand out the food. As is always the case, just when everyone is really busy and the food trolley is in the centre of the main room, an emergency patient is brought through and everything is in the way. Amy dropped the post on the side of the nurses' station and got into action. It is a young patient in their teens admitted to A and E with complaints of abdominal pains that had been hurting all night and were getting progressively worse. He is groaning with the pain and Tom rushes out of his consultation room to assist. Soon the boy is transferred from the ambulance stretcher onto the hospital bed and pulled into the consultation bay especially designed for the emergencies near the door. Amy pulled the curtain round the cubicle and Julie joined them. The patient is examined and Tom asks Amy to administer 10 mg of morphine and to request blood and urine samples. He asks Julie to try and contact the next of kin and within minutes the patient is made comfortable. Tom suspected it to be a severe case of appendicitis and suggested the only option may be to operate. Amy phoned ahead to book a slot in theatre in case this is the outcome of the tests.

The rest of the day was less eventful with only ten new admissions and five of the overnight patients were discharged by midday. One new admission was a girl with glass cut wounds after being a passenger in a car that had collided with a tree. Luckily the driver was completely uninjured and it hadn't been any worse. The girl had glass fragments that needed to be removed from her face and arms and Amy spent a good hour and a half carefully removing the shards of glass with tweezers. The girl was called Tammy, only 12 years old and so brave. By the time 7.30 pm rolled around Amy was exhausted and as always ready to call it a day and head home for a good soak in the bath.

Chapter 7

Michael

Face book status – just bought a new lens for the camera awesome shots

Michael has been with his girlfriend for the past 8 years. They met at a wedding for one of his friends he had met at university in Falmouth. Emma was one of the bridesmaids and the moment he saw her walking behind the bride in her brown flowing dress he knew he had to be with her. He didn't even know her name but she had golden blonde curly hair down to her shoulders and the most stunning smile it was love at first sight.

They had moved in together after 2 years of dating and 6 years on they are at the crossroads of where to go next. Would Michael propose? His job means he works odd hours and often photographs evening and weekend functions such as weddings, birthday parties, balls as well as day time work in a shop he rents from another photographer in the nearby town of Sandgate. He earns a lot when there is work but it is fluctual and some weeks can be very quiet while others are jammed pack of appointments. Emma is a secretary for a local building company. They have had their ups and downs and currently there are financial worries which are causing a continuing friction in their relationship.

Emma is at work and it is midday. She logs out of her computer and heads to the canteen for lunch. Meanwhile Michael has no work mid week and he has finished processing the photographs and sent them off to the printers. Time for the pub he thinks and within ten minutes he is sat on his favourite bar stool with the old locals chatting about how things used to be in their day.

Michael has issues with his mum. He is a very successful photographer but for some reason she doesn't approve of such a faddy career. It makes him feel worthless and as if he is not good enough. He tries to speak to her about it but she just changes the subject and offers him a coffee or a cup of tea. His mum thinks he has a drink problem. He thinks his mum is interfering and neurotic. When really all they do is care about each other.

7.30pm

Amy has just got home from work and she walks into a lovely warm house. She takes off her gloves and boots and puts her coat on the hook, she gives her mum and dad a hug and they ask her how her day was. There is a lovely quaint fireplace lit and candles around it. They all sit by the fire and talk about their days at work. Amy has offered to cook the dinner and she cooks mussels for starter, chicken for main course and lemon cheesecake for dessert. It is a success and everyone loves it.

After dinner once the food has gone down they decide not to watch TV for a change and instead they play a game of trivial pursuit. Amy has never been any good at general knowledge and so she asks the questions and her mum and dad have to answer them.

'Who is the current prime minister?' Amy asks.

'Tony Blair' Her dad guesses wrongly.

'Is it John Major?' Her mum guesses wrongly.

'Nooo, Its David Cameron' Amy says with a laugh.

'Next question' Her mum orders.

'Ok, give me a moment mum' Amy chides with a smile.

'What is the capital of Spain?' Amy asks.

'Madrid' Her dad answers.

'Yes great, well done dad' Amy responds.

'Where is the Eiffel tower?' Amy asks.

'Paris' her mum answers with glee at getting the right answer.

'Well done darling' Amy's dad congratulates her mum with a kiss.

'What is the capital of New Zealand?' Amy asks.

'I can't remember' Amy's mum replies.

'It is Wellington' her dad answers.

'When was apartheid abolished in South Africa?' Amy asks.

'I have no idea' her mum replies.

'In 1991' her dad answers. 'The last of the pillars of apartheid were abolished. It means that everyone has equal opportunity now.'

'Oh well done darling you are so clever' Amy's mum responds.

'Who is the president of the United States?' Amy asks.

'Barack Obama' Amy's dad responds.

'What date was independence day?' Amy asks.

'July the 4th' Amy's mum replies.

'Very knowledgeable' Amy says.

They finish the game and hug each other good night.

Chapter 8

Zoe

Face book status – Can't wait to go out for dinner with Amy tonight yay!

It is Wednesday and Amy has just finished another busy shift at the hospital. Today was different because instead of heading home for her tea and a bath she would be going straight out for dinner with her old friend Zoe. They were meeting just down the road from the hospital in Tasha's, a funky bar/restaurant that served delicious Thai food. Amy has a quick shower in the staff changing rooms and is walking her way to the restaurant just 15 minutes later. She had met her friend Zoe on a work placement when she had first moved to the area. Zoe worked as a District nurse and had helped Amy train when she was finishing her studies. The two girls were inseparable ever since they met and would meet religiously once a week for dinner. Amy found Zoe sat at their table ready with a menu in hand and gave her a quick hug.

"Hi Zoe, how are you my dear?" Amy greeted her.

"Hi Amy I'm good thanks apart from absolutely exhausted from work but what is new there?" Zoe replied.

"I know, I feel exactly the same, relentless isn't it?" Amy said.

"Ah but I wouldn't change jobs for the world though." Zoe said.

"No your right, all this hand holding is good for the soul" Amy laughed.

"Hand holding?" Zoe questioned.

" Ah maybe I should explain, ever since I told Matt I was a nurse he has called the profession holding hands and that has kind of stuck a chord with me ever since, I think it is a good way to describe what we do, a very affectionate term. It kind of makes it sound rewarding and well, just worthwhile." Amy explained.

"Yeah I get it; I never thought of it as that before, only ever in the romantic way but I suppose it makes sense in a nursing context too. Although in reality it is mostly cleaning up sick, pooh and blood." Zoe replied and laughed.

Amy laughed in agreement. "Very True".

They ordered their food and some wine and continued chatting about work and their lack of love lives for the next two hours before they both realised the time and that they had work the next day and must head off home.

16

10pm

Alex and Ollie just entered the bar as two rather good looking mid-twenties girls were walking out. Shame, Ollie thought, they would have been great to strike up a conversation with. Even so, he flashed a cheeky forward smile at them as they crossed paths and he realised he was already just a little bit drunk. Alex and Ollie had started drinking back at Alex's bachelor pad a few hours before and then only headed out around 10pm. They reached the bar and Alex got a round in, comprising of two lagers and two shots of Jägermeister for good measure. Alex is 27 and a recently qualified architect, he had worked hard to get where he was and he works for a local successful firm of architects. He has his own flat and enjoys the single life to the limit. His best friend Ollie is an accountant but he still lives at home with his parents. He is still saving for a mortgage in order to move out. Alex and Ollie like a drink and loved their nights out on the town. They stayed in Tasha's bar for another 3 rounds and it was midnight by the time they thought about making a move and were far too drunk to realise they had outstayed their welcome in the now empty bar.

12.04pm

As they leave the bar and get outside onto the pavement beside the road Alex takes a look at his watch and discovers it is just past 12 pm. He surprises himself how sober he feels and decides to convince Ollie that it would be so much cheaper if he just drove them home. After all he had driven his car down here no problem and it would be a nuisance to have to come back tomorrow and collect it. Ollie hesitates and even in his inebriated condition finds the common sense to try and persuade Alex it just isn't a good idea. He says 'Mate, I am so drunk there is no way you aren't as well, maybe we should just get a taxi home' and places an arm around Alex's shoulders. Alex shrugs the arm off and turns to face Ollie, he says 'I'm sober - honest mate, I only had a few, I'll be fine, come on it'll save us about £20 and we don't have to queue at the taxi rank.'

12.45pm

A and E have just had a call to warn them of two new casualties due in to the ward shortly. A driver has crashed his car into a traffic island on a notoriously narrow part of one of the local roads. Reports suggest the driver was drunk and suffering with heavy bleeding from a head injury. There was also the passenger, obviously drunk as well and who was suffering superficial injuries such as cuts and concussion. The staff prepare the emergency cubicles and in 10 minutes they have both the victims admitted and treatment commenced. There is a lot of blood from the head injury and the man is unconscious. He also has broken ribs and is having difficulty breathing so the staff have had to put him on a ventilator to stabilise him. It is looking to be quite serious and his next of kin are contacted quickly.

The passenger on the other hand had it seemed to have a lucky escape. He is patched up and would be observed over night to make sure that it was only slight concussion. The fact he was drunk made it harder to keep the patient awake whilst he was observed and the patient had been sick several times. Julie is on shift and has been involved in caring for both the patients. She is shocked at how drunk the driver must have been to collide with a traffic island. Drink driving incidents were quite high and it always seemed to end up with at least one head injury. The driver is eventually stabilised, taken off the ventilator and after a few hours he starts to regain consciousness, still evidently drunk he isn't making much sense. The bleeding is heavy because alcohol thins the blood and it made for a hard job to control it. Julie has to continuously replace the bandages until the blood started to clot and it is eventually under control. He has lost a considerable amount of blood. It appears that the head injury looked worse than it was and by the early hours of the morning the doctors have established there is no brain damage and apart from broken ribs, severe bruising, cuts and a big headache, the patient is stable and moved to another cubicle to sleep off the rest of his drunkenness. Needless to say he was very sick and Julie was there to deal with this and observe him as he started to sober up.

Thursday 8am

The parents have turned up during the night only to find their son and his friend both asleep and recovering. They have been briefed by the doctor and the policeman told them that the men had crashed in to a traffic island and that Alex had been drink driving. It almost caused Mrs Craig, Alex's mother to faint with shock when she had learnt of this. Too ashamed to speak, her husband continued the discussion with them and found out that their son had had a narrow escape from a head injury and that he should be fine. They waited until Alex would wake up and sat at his bedside wracked with worry. Alex eventually woke up in a daze and immediately raised his hand to his head, what was that pain? Then he took in his surroundings and through the blur could just about make out the silhouette of his mum and dad starring back at him. His head was pounding and he had memories of being sick and then he remembered the crash and suddenly felt very sick all over again. His mum said nothing but just started crying and his dad moved towards the bed and held Alex's hand. Alex tried to speak but his chest hurt and he lost his breath. Eventually he could speak and just said "What happened?"
His dad let go of his hand and replied "At least you are ok son. You crashed your car and it seems you were very drunk. We'll talk about that later, for now just get some rest."
With this he turned to comfort his wife and Alex slipped back into a deeply hung-over and pained sleep.

Down the corridor Ollie's parents were sat at his bedside and Ollie was awake and sitting up, Julie the nurse had done his observations and given him the all clear to go home. The policeman had also finished taking his statement and Ollie's parents helped Ollie up and out of bed and they made there way slowly to the car and home.

At 7.30am Amy walks through the double doors into the A and E department to take over from Julie and is briefed about the drink driver patient. Alex Craig. 27. Brought in after crashing his car and recovering from a head injury, heavily sedated and only just sobering up. Julie informs Amy that the policemen are waiting in the relatives' room in order to take a statement from the patient once he is rested, sober and coherent.

Later that day during her break Amy picks up the local newspaper and the front page article reads clearly: Drunk driver hits traffic island and escapes serious head injury. She scans the article and can make out that the young man is making a full recovery and it is likely he will lose his licence and have to attend a drink awareness course. It doesn't say whether he will go to jail or not but Amy thinks seeing as no one else was seriously injured he might just get away with a community service order. Perhaps he'll have to fix the broken traffic island she mused. The article ends with a note stating how lucky both the driver and passenger were because they weren't more seriously injured.

Chapter 9

Matt

Face book Status – Enjoyed the bag of chips and walk along the beach

It is the second week of December and Matt is meeting Amy from a shift at the hospital and they go for chips on the sea front. Matt asks how holding hands is going? This is his affectionate term he uses to refer to her profession of being a nurse. It is a week since Alex Craig had been brought in from the car crash incident and he had only been discharged this afternoon. Amy tells Matt about the drink driver incident.

"We had quite a serious case in this week, a guy named Alex Craig. He was drink driving and he crashed into a traffic reservation and he and his friend ended up in A and E". Amy told him.

"Oh yeah mum told me about that, he read about it in the newspaper. It was that traffic island just down by that antiques shop on the coast road, do you know where I mean?" Matt asked.

"I know where you mean, I drove past it this morning, and they still haven't repaired it. Actually come to think of it you might know his friend who was in the passenger seat, his name was Ollie?" Amy replied.

"Ollie Fergus?" Matt replied.
"Yeah, that's him... Don't worry he just had cuts and bruise thankfully. They were so lucky; apparently they were going really fast." Amy said.

"I can't believe it, I play football with him. I'm glad he is ok. Drink drivers ey, a bit silly really." Matt said.

"Yeah they sure are, we get about 5 drink driving related injuries a month at work, it's so bad, and we had one death last month. A girl who was only 16 and to make matters worse her boyfriend was the driver. Imagine that guilt you would have to live with." Amy said.

"That's awful" Matt said. They sat in thoughtful silence and ate their chips.

Later that night Matt picks up the days paper, another article has an update on the driving incident and it explains that the driver was a 27 year old architect named Alex Craig. He has lost his licence and is due in court next Monday. It is also reported that he has lost his job and it isn't looking bright for the man.

Chapter 10

Amy

Face book status – Can't believe it is only a week until Xmas woohoo!

It's nearly Christmas time. The 18th of December and Matt is helping Amy buy a Christmas tree for her cousins, Lily and Ben. Sally their mum was too busy at the after school PTA meeting about funding and has asked Amy to do it. Amy loves to babysit her cousins and it is her day off so she went to collect them from school at 3.30pm. They met Matt at the garden centre in town and are now currently sizing up the Christmas trees trying to find a suitable one. Matt is holding up a giant Christmas tree and making Lily laugh by comparing its' tall height to Lily's height.
'It's so tall' shrieked Lily, with all the excitement, even at 15 years old Christmas still seemed magical.
'It is twice the size of you' replied Matt as he put the tree down and tried to find a less imposing one. 'How about this?' he suggests to Lily. 'Do you think it would fit in your living room?'

'Erm, yes I think it would' said Lily.
'What do you think Ben?' Matt asked trying to include him in on the decision.

'Yeah, that'll do just fine' replied Ben, who was much more preoccupied with the nearby cactuses to really have any idea to offer. Ben is 12 years old and like most boys his age has the attention span of a fish.

'Ok this is the one please' said Amy to the garden centre assistant, who was waiting patiently behind them.

Soon the Christmas tree was all wrapped with netting and a lot less bushy in order to transport it home. Matt and Ben carried it out to the car and took at least 10 minutes trying to squash it down so it would fit. Lily and Amy queued up to pay and bought Lily's mum a small pot plant as a present.

'Can we go and get some hot chocolate now please?' asked an eager and suggesting Lily.

'Ok then, seeing as you asked so nicely' smiled Amy.

They all clambered into the overcrowded car and headed off to a café down the road. The café was very busy and Ben ever the cheeky one, managed to jump into an empty set of sofas that had just been vacated by some leaving customers. They ordered hot chocolate for Ben and Lily and tea for Ryan and Amy. Once all comfortably sat, the conversation turned to school and Lily and Bens' friends and before they new it they had been chatting for an hour.

'Ok guys, let's get you home, it's nearly dinner time and your mum should be back from her meeting by now.' Amy explained.

Sally has just left the PTA meeting and is exhausted. All the parents, having their say and so many opinions and matters to discuss. Sometimes she wonders how she manages her job because it is so demanding. When she arrives home, on the drive, are her two smiling children and what looks like a giant tree. She sees Amy and Matt sat on the doorstep all wrapped up in their winter coats and gloves.
'Oh Amy, I hope you lot haven't been waiting long it's getting very cold outside?' Sally worried.
'No we only just unloaded the car, no worries.' Replied Amy.
'Ah yes, the Christmas tree - how wonderful, thank you Matt and Amy, that has saved me a job and isn't it magnificent?' Sally said.

'Isn't it great?' said Lily and greeted her mum. 'We took ages to decide and then we went and got hot chocolate!' She described.

'Oh lovely' Said Sally. 'Well thanks again you two, do you want to stay for dinner?' Sally offered.

'Thanks Aunt Sally but I must be going as mum would have already cooked me dinner but definitely another time.' Amy replied hoping Matt wouldn't be offended by her decline.

'Yeah the same goes for me' said Matt, as if reading Amy's mind and making his excuses.

And with that Sally and the children went inside into the warm and Matt drove Amy home.

Chapter 11

Sally

The Nativity Play

It is the night of the school nativity play the school hall has tinsel and decorations everywhere. There are Christmas songs playing out of the stereo. Sally is rushing around organizing all the children to make sure they have their costumes and the parents are starting to arrive in the school hall. The parents are all settling into their seats and they have their cameras ready to take photos of their children who they are so proud of. The lights are turned down and everyone hushes and waits for the play to begin. The curtains draw open and there is applause from the audience as they wait in anticipation for the first scene.

A star appears on the stage it is a child dressed as a star. Everyone laughs. He walks from the left to the right of the stage and disappears. Then the three wise men walk across the stage and say they are following the star to Bethlehem.

Then the next scene shows Mary and Joseph walking to Bethlehem looking for somewhere to have the baby. They are tired and have been walking for days and days.

The next scene is Mary and Joseph knocking at an Inn. The innkeeper says there is no room at the inn. They keep walking around the stage and knock at another inn. The innkeeper says there is no room but there is a stable out the back and they can stay there.

The curtains close. And the children gather on the stage in their places. The children start to sing Away in a Manger.

The curtains open and the stage is set as the stable. There is straw on the floor and Mary is cradling a baby. Joseph has his arm around Mary. Jesus has been born and there are Angels, Shepherds, sheep, cows, a donkey and everyone sings Silent night. Sally applauses with pride when she sees Hannah the Angel and Stuart as the Wiseman, they sing so beautifully.

The curtains close and all the parents applause.

The curtains open again and the children sing We Wish you a Happy Christmas and A Happy New Year.

Some parents are crying with happiness at their sweet lovely children and there is a standing ovation.

Chapter 12

Matt

Face book status – is looking forward to some much needed time off work

Matt has arranged to go around to dinner with his brother Michael. He arrives early and has brought a bottle of red wine. As he walks up the narrow path to the small house his brother owns he can hear raised voices. He slows his pace and leans forward to hear what is going on. He can hear Emma's voice saying something along the lines of 'I've just had enough you never tell me where you are and I worry when you don't get in until 7am the next morning. Is it so much to ask for a text or a phone call to let me know that you are safe?' Her voice sounded hollow and desolate. Then Michael spoke in a loud and angry voice. 'Oh for god's sake I can't do anything without having to tell you where I am, who I'm with and when I'm going to be home. Who do you think you are my probation officer?

Silence. A door slammed and Matt realized that there were rushed footsteps coming towards the front door so he panicked and pressed the door bell so as to not appear conspicuous and as if he had been obviously eves-dropping. Emma flung the door open and looked flustered as she saw Matt standing in front of her and clearly in her way. She was in no mood to stop her intentions of walking out but felt obliged to greet Matt and felt guilt because she had just cooked the three of them dinner which was currently probably burning on the hot plate.
'Hey Emma' Matt offered the bottle of wine forward in an attempt to appear normal.
'Matt, hi, I'm really sorry but I'm not staying for dinner. Change of plans, its all ready to be served in the kitchen. Got to go!' She had tears in her eyes and brushed past in determination to get away.
Matt stood frozen to the spot trying to decide if he should go after her or go in and see his brother, he decided he had better not make the situation worse and brushed his shoes on the mat as he closed the door behind him.
'Hey Michael, is everything ok bro?' Matt asked.
'Hi Matt, yeah it's fine. Women ey.' Michael slumped down on the couch. 'Oh good you've got some wine just what I need right now. Crack it open glasses are in one of the cupboards somewhere. What's that smell?' Michael jumped up and ran into the kitchen the risotto that Emma had been cooking for the last hour was now a black mass in the pan.
'Great, guess its pizza takeout then?' Michael smirked at Matt. They both peered over the saucepan to survey the damage and then nodded in agreement.
'So... what was that all about then?' Matt decided to tackle the issue head on, it was none of his business but he and Michael were quite close and it looked like he might need to talk.
They opened the wine and ordered the pizza before they sat down in the cosy living room and Michael then prompted to turn the football on and change the subject as if nothing had happened.

He was drinking the glass of wine as if it was water taking large gulps and within 2 minutes it had been demolished. Matt had barely taken two sips. Must have been a bad argument thought Matt.

Later on, Michael turns the TV off and talks to Matt. 'I'm just so worried about Emma. She is always cleaning the house and going to the gym and whenever we are both together all we do is argue.' Michael says.

'You argue all the time?' Matt asks.

'Well, no, that's not true. We watch TV together and sometimes go for bikes rides.' Michael admits.

'Well that has to be good then, just try talking to each other rather than watching TV all the time.' Matt suggests.

'Good advice brother.' Michael smiles and they have a manly hug.

Chapter 13

Amy

Face book status – Wants to know who Zoe's going on a date with!

The next day Amy is up and out of bed at 6.30 am ready to start her new week of shifts at work. It is the start of the Christmas holidays and only 1 week to go before Christmas and unfortunately for Amy this means not very much to her as the Christmas holidays are just as busy as any other time of year at the hospital. Amy is just an hour into her shift when they receive a new patient, a cancer victim called Bridget Deegan who has come in with problems due to side effects of her chemotherapy. As a side effect of chemotherapy treatment, it lowers the immune system and it is very common that patients pick up infections and this is what has happened with Bridget's case. She is very poorly and needs antibiotic treatment as soon as possible to stop the infection getting worse and spreading. She is quickly admitted to the ward and put on the right antibiotics to fight the infection and Amy is in charge of keeping close observations on her.

'Morning the beautiful Amy' Jake greets her as he enters the cubicle to assist her with the observations.

Bridget, the patient, despite being very unwell cracks a smile at this comment and Amy looks up in alarm to see Jake grinning back at her.

'Morning Jake' Amy replies unsure how else to respond. 'How are you today?' she adds.

'Oh just great thanks' Jake replies ever so cheerfully. 'Here to help as always' and he got to work with the temperature reading.

Later on that day as Amy is seeing to another patient, Jake, once again pops his head round the curtain and smiles keenly before walking off whistling along his way. Amy thinks this is very odd and starts to wonder why Jake is being so friendly. On her lunch break Amy phones Zoe and has a quick chat about how they are and when they are due to next meet up. She also tells Zoe about her unwanted attention from Jake, the nursing assistant and Zoe laughs in hysterics. It would seem Amy had herself an admirer. They agree to meet that night at Amys' parents' house for dinner.

Amy gets home at 8pm and can smell the cooking as she walks through the front door. 'Mmm yum, that smells good mum.' She shouts through to the kitchen.
'Through here love, Zoe is already here and we've got chilli con carne for dinner' her mum replied. They all sit down to eat and catch up on the days events.

Later Zoe and Amy sit in the privacy of the conservatory.
'Sooo, how is it going with your new boyfriend Jake?' Zoe teases Amy.
'Ha-ha you are not funny' responds Amy. 'He is so over friendly, it is embarrassing'. Amy explains.

'Ha-ha sounds like you got yourself a good catch there then' Zoe giggled.
'No I'm serious, I wouldn't be surprised if he leans in for a hug tomorrow.'
The door bell went.

Matt has popped over with a new cycle route booklet he has downloaded from the council website.

'Hi Zoe, how are you?' Matt greets Zoe after giving Amy the booklet.
'Good thanks' Zoe replies and they continue chatting about work and how they saw each other out the other night in a bar in town. They share a private joke about the local who fell off his stall and they are both consumed with laughter over this. Amy can't help but notice some chemistry between Zoe and Matt and surprises herself when she feels a tinge of jealousy. She laughs to try and join in but doesn't really share the hilarity.
'Would you like to stay for a cup of tea?' Amy offers Matt.
'No thanks Ames, I'm off to play football in half an hour so best head off.' Matt replies and they say their good byes.

Amy re-enters the conservatory after seeing Matt out of the front door, and says to Zoe 'So you and Matt were out together the other night then, I didn't know that?' there is a slight accusatory tone to her voice.
'No not out together, we just bumped into each other that's all.' Zoe replies a little defensively.
'Oh right.' Amy replies. 'Would you erm, like be interested in Matt then?' Amy questioned.
'Oh Amy, no, don't be ridiculous, he'd never go after me and besides that isn't even an issue as I have a hot date tomorrow night!' Zoe responded and swiftly changed the subject.
'Really, a date ey?' Amy teases, glad to be off the topic of Matt. 'Yes a real life, official, date.' Zoe replies.
'Wow, who with?' Amy asks.
'Just someone, its early days so I'm not going to say' Zoe says.
'Oh that's not fair, you have to tell me!' Amy smiles.
'No way, but I promise I'll phone you after and tell you all the details about how it went.' Zoe offers by way of a compromise.
'Ok, if that's all I'm going to get, I'll have to settle for that.' Amy concedes.
They chat into the night and Zoe leaves around 11pm.

Chapter 14

Chloe

Face book status – Is looking forward to the Xmas party tonight! Roll on 6pm.

Sally and Sue are out for their Thursday night meet. It is only one week until Christmas and they have both just finished their Christmas shopping at the late night shopping centre. They are in a local wine bar just a few minutes away from the shopping centre and it is the first time they have been here. The bar is called Rene's and it is very stylish, with brown and black leather sofas and cream walls. There are glass vases on the tables with white roses in them. It is a lovely little place to enjoy a glass of wine and unwind away from their hectic family lives. They sit and discuss the presents they have bought and how successful the trip has been. There conversation switches to the lovely taste of the wine they are drinking and they discuss their favourite tipples.
Sally says 'Talking of alcohol, my Lily has started to discover the world of vodka and wine, she is only 14 can you believe it?'
'Well, yes I can believe it really' replies Sue. 'My Michael has already been to two early Christmas parties held round a friends' house while the parents were away and he asked if he could take a crate of John's beer!' 'Of course we said no and that he was too young.'
Sally explains she is worried that her 14 year old Lily has started wearing short skirts to parties and thinks she is drinking too much already. 'Last Sunday she spent nearly all day in bed with a hangover, I couldn't believe how many hours she slept for.' Sally complained.
'Well weren't we the same at their age?' Sue pondered. 'No actually thinking about it, we weren't that young.' Sue decided.

It is Thursday evening in Central London and the week before Christmas. Chloe is out at a Christmas party with people from work. The bar is just off Oxford Street and a few streets away from there office. About 20 people from work are here with their various other halves and friends of friends have all been invited. Some people have tinsel wrapped around their necks and there are tasteful fairy lights decorated around the minimalistic bar walls. The music is playing Mariah Careys' 'All I want for Christmas is You' and people are merrily singing along. It is a great atmosphere and the drinks are flowing. Chloe has been caught talking to her ever so dull boss and is nodding along dutifully as he tells her about his planned Christmas vacation in Tuscany. She on the other hand is looking forward to a nice winter break in Val de sere skiing over the Christmas week with a friend. If he would just stop talking for one minute she would tell him this but it's a one way conversation and Chloe has to stifle a yawn. She eventually makes her excuses and joins her office friends back at the bar for another round and the night rolls round into the early hours of the next day. She gets in at about 1 am and falls straight into bed.

Chapter 15
Amy

Face book status – is annoyed...

It's Saturday morning and Matt and Amy go for a cycle on the usual coastal route they always take. It is a brisk cold morning and they have had to wrap up warm. Despite the cold, the sky is bright blue and the winter sun is shining brightly. After about half an hour they stop at a bench and sit down for a rest. Amy starts to tell Matt about her work colleague Jake and how yesterday he had asked her out on a date. Matt laughs as Amy describes how much she is not interested in Jake in that way and how she had to make up an elaborate excuse as to what she was doing this evening instead.

Matt changes his face to a serious frown and says 'Maybe you should give him a chance and live a little?' Amy takes offence and sits in silence. What does he mean by live a little, I live quite well thank you very much. Then she decides to lighten the air and teases 'Well I don't see you going on many dates either!' Matt laughs but can't help than feel a bit annoyed.

He finally replies 'That may be true but I'm busy with work and football, you know what its like. Anyway you never go out; all you do since you left uni in London is work and go home, why don't you let down your hair a little and go on a date? What is the worse that could happen?'

'Excuse me, I do go out!' Argues Amy with a sharp tone to her voice. She doesn't like where this conversation is leading.

'Ok, ok sorry maybe that was a bit harsh' Matt concedes. 'I just think maybe dating someone could be good for you; you know, meet someone new, open up a bit?' Matt suggests.

Amy replies 'Open up a bit? What do you mean by that?'

'Well ... its just you are a bit of a closed book.' Matt says.

Amy is really annoyed now 'A closed book? No I'm not.'

Matt explains 'Erm, you kind of are... you never talk about your past, about your time in London.'
        Amy is silent, he has touched a nerve. Matt nudges her arm 'Hey, its ok if you don't want to talk about it I understand, I'm sorry I shouldn't have brought this up.'
Amy turns to look at Matt and her face is a sight for sore eyes 'Ok, lets just change the subject.' And with that they get back on their bikes in awkward silence and head back home.

It's Saturday afternoon and Matt and Ollie are out for a drink after football. Matt tells Ollie about the slight argument he had had with Amy earlier that day. Matt and Ollie aren't that close friends, they just play football together and Matt finds telling someone that doesn't know Amy well about the argument strangely comforting.

Matt explains how frustrated he feels that Amy has this whole 4 years that she spent in London that she never talks about and whenever he asks she just clams up. Ollie suggests that maybe it just isn't anything to worry about. Matt disagrees and says 'there is definitely a story to tell' and he is worried that she will never trust him enough to tell him. Ollie teases Matt that he is overly concerned and maybe Matt has romantic interests for Amy.

The conversation changes and they talk about Alex, Ollie's' friend who was driving the car the night of the accident. Ollie says 'Did you know he lost his license and is facing a charge'.

'Yeah that's awful' Matt replies.

'It was a horrible experience that's for sure' Ollie says and he frowns with the memory of it all.

'So glad you both came out of it ok and well' Matt says. 'Let's hope he gets let off the charge and learns his lesson. There is a good chance he will if it's his first offence' Matt reassures and this is comfort to Ollie. They finish up their drinks and head off to the showers.

Amy has just turned on the news. There has been an earthquake in Haiti. She cannot believe the devastation she is witnessing on the television screen. It looks like most of the city and the surrounding area has been affected with thousands of people homeless and lots of people injured and dead. All the buildings have collapsed and they are still experiencing after shock tremors. This is unbelievable Amy thinks.

Chapter 16

Michael

Face book status - banging night!

Michael is currently laying in bed and it is 2pm. He got in at 4am this morning and has the worst hangover of his life. He cannot lift his head from the pillow and although he needs a glass of water there is no energy left to go and get one. Emma has gone out to the gym and so he can't even shout to her to get him some water. This is the lowest point of his life he thinks to himself. I had so much to do today such as cook Emma breakfast, cut the lawn and visit his grandparents. Its only Saturday though, he consoles himself, I can do it all tomorrow.

Emma is currently down the gym, she is running fast on the treadmill. She pounds away to the music and tries to fight back the tears. She cannot believe Michael went out again last night with his mates and just left her at home. He didn't even think to invite her. She knows men need their space and time out with their mates but all the same he never considers her feelings. He rolled in drunk at about 4am this morning and threw up in the toilet. So attractive thought Emma. She had to laugh though; she loved him all the same. He just doesn't have any limits and drinks alcohol as if it is water. Emma tries to think about something else, it's very difficult to though when you care about someone and you are watching the person you love throwing their life away.

They have a cooked breakfast together and all is forgiven. They start the day with a walk through the woods near where they live and the weather is lovely outside. The leaves on the trees sway with the wind. It is so peaceful.

Chapter 17

Amy

Face book status – is no longer annoyed

Zoe and Amy are on the phone.
'Can you believe what happened in Haiti?' Amy asks Zoe.
'I know, it's terrible!' Zoe agrees.
'The news was so scary to watch just imagine being there…' Amy thought.
'Yeah, those poor people.' Zoe says. 'Anyway enough of bad news, I have good news too…' Zoe begins.
'So I've started seeing the guy I went on a date with!' Zoe exclaims happily.
'Oh wow that's great' Amy replies. 'Who is he? What's his name?' She adds.
'I'm still not telling you that.' Zoe says defiantly.
'Ah that's not fair!' Amy moans.
'Well its early days yet and I don't want to jinx it' Zoe explains.
'Ok miss secretive, we'll just call him Mr X for now' Amy said.

'So what's new with you?' Zoe asks.
'Well not much really except me and Matt had a little bit of an argument the other day and I haven't seen him since.' Amy said.
'Why what happened?' Asked Zoe.
'Well, he challenged me about the fact I didn't want to go out with Jake for a date this weekend. He said I never go out any more and then started going on about how I don't open up to anyone and he asked me why I never talk about my years in London.' Amy explained.
'Oh' Zoe said. 'That had to be a bit awkward, what did you say to him?' Zoe asked.
'Not much, I just got defensive and said that I did go out and was just silent for a while.' Amy replied.
'I see, well I'm sure you'll see him soon and it will all be forgotten about.' Zoe conceded.
'Yeah I hope your right' Amy said. 'I really don't want the subject of London to come up again'.
'Yeah, well maybe it would do you good to tell someone apart from me about all that.' Zoe suggested.
Amy went silent again and then Zoe had to change the subject to get her talking again.
Amy just said 'I'm not ready to talk about it with anyone.' And that was the subject matter closed.

Later that night Matt texted Amy and asked if she wanted to go to the cinema. When they have parked the car and are walking towards the complex, Matt stops abruptly and tugs Amy's' sleeve.

'I'm really sorry about the other night' he says. 'I said some stuff I shouldn't have and pushed you to talk about something that you obviously aren't comfortable about. So yeah I'm really sorry Ames.' Matt apologises.

Amy turns to look up at Matt and smiles. 'That's ok, I'm sorry for being so moody. Can we just forget about it?' Amy replies.
They both smile and nod and Matt leans in to give Amy a hug. Amy is slightly taken aback because this is something Matt has never done before and she feels the warmth of his body, it feels nice and very familiar. They hug for a bit longer than necessary and then Amy says 'We better go inside or we'll miss the film.'

When they get out of the cinema around 11pm, Matt finds he has 3 missed calls on his mobile which he had turned off during the film. He pauses and presses the number for his answer phone; Amy hops around on the pavement trying to prevent the cold getting to her feet. Matt's face suddenly falls and he looks very concerned and pale. He finally finishes the call and just stares in shock at Amy.
'What's wrong?' Amy asks and moves forward towards him.
'It's my brother' Matt can only reply. He looks close to tears.
'What about your brother?' Amy asks softly.
'He's been rushed into hospital with problems with his Liver. He's really ill apparently. Can we go to the hospital to see him?' Matt asks.
'Of course, I'll drive you there now.' Amy says and off they went.

Chapter 18

Chloe

Face book status – Holiday time woohoo!

Chloe is on holiday with her friend Clare from work. They are staying in a hotel in the centre of Val D'Isere. They spend every day skiing on the sun drenched slopes and all night partying in the local bars. It is Wednesday the day after Boxing Day and they have just finished skiing for the day. It is traditional when you finish your last ski run to have 'Après Ski' in the bar at the bottom of the slope. The bar is open aired and has lively euro pop music blaring out. They order two beers and get chatting to some tanned hunky looking locals at the bar. Chloe is talking to a guy called Pier. He is typically French looking except for the string of onions and the striped t-shirt. They hit it off and spend the evening chatting and before the night has finished Chloe can be found in the corner of the bar kissing Pier. Clare tells Chloe she is heading back to the hotel, now very fed up at being stuck talking to Pier's friends for the last few hours. Chloe nods in acknowledgement and says she'll be back a bit later as she is going to stay for another drink. Pier's friend mutters something in French to Pier and sets off home as well, having clearly got the message that three is a crowd.

Pier goes and buys them another drink and they continue to get to know each other, chatting drunken nonsense and staring gooey eyed into each others eyes in between kissing. It gets to 1 am and the bar is shutting for the night. Chloe knows she should go back to the hotel but she really likes Pier and doesn't want the night to end. She has had plenty to drink and would concede yes, she is very drunk. She is feeling rather attracted to him and it is clear Pier would like her to go back with him to his room. The decision is made in the instant he kisses her again. He has such soft lifts and as he holds her up to leave she feels his defined muscles through the sleeve of his shirt. They stagger round the corner to his rather posh hotel and make there way up in the lift to his room. Before the lift even arrives on the right floor they are already kissing passionately in the lift. As the door pings and opens they almost fall through the opening and have to steady themselves up as they walk down the corridor. Chloe has taken her shoes off and is giggling nervously. They get into the room and clothes are all over the floor in a matter of seconds. The next morning Chloe wakes up and wonders where the hell she is.

Chapter 19

Lily

'Be home by 10 ok?' Sally shouts after Lily as she skips out of the house in no more than a belt for a skirt and luckily a winter coat to cover her top half at least.
'Yeah' Lily shouts back at the house as she runs down the garden path. Her friend is waiting in her parent's car to give her a lift to the Christmas party. It is 7pm and the party has already started. The girls are so excited and can't stop talking in high pitched squeals the whole journey there. They finally arrive 5 minutes later. Jessie's mum tells her to be home by 10 too and thinks she can hear the clink of drink bottles in the suspicious carrier bag her daughter is carrying as she gets out of the car. Oh well, there isn't much she can do to stop them drinking at the party and at least it will be something they brought themselves she thinks.

The party is round Belle's house, the most popular girl in school and the whole year is here it seems. Lily and Jessie go straight to the kitchen to unload their alcohol and pour themselves a first drink. They have a bottle of vodka and a bottle of lemonade between them. The music is blaring out J-Z and it is going to be a good night. Lily has never drunk Vodka before and finds it to be rather strong tasting. She gags as she tries to swallow the neat mixture and has to add more lemonade to get rid of the horrible taste.
A few hours later and there are about 100 pretty drunk 15 year olds shouting the words along to Kings of Leon 'Sex on fire'. Everyone is having the time of their lives. Lily turns to see who just spilt a drink on her back and as she does everything seems to blur. She thinks she better sit down and perch herself onto the arm of a sofa. As she goes to step towards the sofa she trips on the culprit's foot and ends up falling onto the lap of the most gorgeous boy she has ever seen, Tom. Oh the embarrassment. She slurs her apology and tries to get up, he has to push her off him and she just stands there with the world spinning around her.
Jessie comes over and asks her if she is alright. 'I don't feel so good' Lily whispers in her drunken state. It is at this moment that she feels extremely dizzy and collapses on the floor in a lump. Jessie screams and bends over her friend in hysteria. Luckily for them Tom who was still sat on the sofa nearby hadn't been drinking and took hold of the situation, picking up Lily in his arms and taking her out of the crowded living room and into the empty bathroom down the corridor. Lily by this point is coming round and says she is going to be sick. She is sick in the toilet and then just slumps against the wall and loses consciousness again. Tom says that he thinks they should call an ambulance. Jessie is by the door crying. They call an ambulance and it arrives in just 10 minutes. Tom tells Jessie to call Lily's' parents and wait at the party to be picked up and that he would go with Lily in the ambulance.

Amy is working the night shift at A and E, it has been unusually quiet for a Friday night and she is just in the staff room making a cup of tea when she hears the double doors open and the hurry of the ambulance crew bringing in a new case. She drops what

she is doing and rushes out to meet the ambulance crew. She can't believe her eyes and does a double take. There lying on the stretcher unconscious with makeup smeared all over her face is her 15 year old cousin Lily. Amy goes into shock and tries to listen to the brief from the paramedic. Apparently she has alcohol poisoning and may need her stomach pumped. It is looking very serious and Amy knows if they don't act quickly this could lead to other complications and Lily could die. David the on call registrar notices the look of shock and fear on Amy's face and immediately asks if she knows the patient. All Amy can do is nod. 'Ok, you aren't to work on this case, call Julie from the bays and you go and get yourself a strong coffee, we'll keep you informed.' David ordered.
Amy just stood there glued to the spot for a moment and then rushed to go and get Julie.

12.05pm

Amy has called Lily's parents and they have just arrived on the ward. Lily has had her stomach pumped but is still unconscious. They are all waiting nervously in the relatives' room. Eventually David the on call doctor pops his head around the door and then opens the door to walk in. He explains that Lily has drunk nearly a bottle of vodka and that although she is feeling very ill and sick still they have pumped her stomach and she is out of the woods. Amy breathes an outwards sigh of relief and says 'Is it ok if we go in and see her?'
'Yes' David replies. 'You can go and see her but she is very poorly and tired out so take it easy on her.' Lily's parents get up and go to Lily's bedside; Sally is holding back the tears as she sees the state of her daughter lying slumped in the hospital bed with a sick bowl next to her chin. Amy checks in to make sure they are all ok then unfortunately has to head back to her shift. She promises to pop by later and see how Lily is getting on.

Later that evening when Amy is in the staff room on her break she sees a poster on the notice board that wasn't there before. It is advertising for volunteer medical staff to go out on a 2 month placement to Haiti with United Nations to help run make shift hospitals for the injured victims of the earthquake. Amy is so taken with the idea she signs her name without thinking twice. Then she realizes this probably isn't the best time to go because of Lily and everything else that has been going on. She reads the small print and it says that the convoy leaves the end of January, which is in two weeks time. Go for it, Amy suddenly thinks, sometimes you just know when you have to do something.

A few days later and it is Tuesday evening, Matt has come round to Amy's house after work to see how Amy is doing.
'Oh hi Matt, how are you?' Amy greets him at the door and Matt steps through into the warm.
'Good thanks, just thought I'd pop by for a cup of tea and a chat.' Matt replies.
They make a cup of tea and go and sit in the conservatory out the back of the house.
'How's your brother?' Amy asks.
'Stable thanks, still in hospital but he is due to be sent home tomorrow. They have told him that in the long term he is going to need a Liver transplant. He has Liver failure.'

Matt explains his voice cracking with emotion.

'Oh that's not good news, I'm so sorry Matt.' Amy comforts him and goes over to give him a hug.

'Thanks, at least he isn't feeling so ill at the moment now he has medication so it could be worse.' Matt says.

'True' Amy agrees.

'Anyway' Matt says 'How is Lily?'

'Oh she is back at home now, they just kept her overnight to observe her and she got the all clear. Silly girl, I can't believe she got into such a state to have to have her stomach pumped. It was such a shock when I saw her brought in on that stretcher, I couldn't believe my eyes.' Amy said.

'I know I bet it was such a shock. I'm glad she is ok.' Matt said.

'Yeah, I doubt she'll be that stupid again' Amy mused.

An hour later and Matt gets up to leave, Amy says she will show him out and when they get to the door they hug again. This is starting to become a bit of a habit thought Amy. It feels good to hug Matt and as Amy pulls away there is a slight hesitation from both sides and they catch each others eyes. It only lasts a split second but they both feel it and then it's as if it never happened. Matt says he had better get off as his mum is getting his dinner on the table. Amy is left standing in the kitchen hall wondering what just happened. She started to busy her mind with making some dinner too.

Chapter 20

Amy

Face book status – Wow that was a long shift, bed time for me!

Amy had some good news today the cancer patient Bridget Deegan has had the all clear to go home and is hopefully going to make a full recovery. Amy is now back at work doing some overtime on Saturday night. She has spent way too much money over Christmas on presents and going out and the overtime is much needed. The only downside is that the overtime is posted on a different ward of the hospital than usual and she has to fill in a shift on the psychiatric ward. Amy has worked a few shifts on this ward before and most of the time it has been quite uneventful and even a bit quiet compared to A and E. She knows it is Saturday night and they might get a new case in off the streets if the police bring someone in. And so it could be quite eventful yet.

One hour into the shift and Amy is looking through the patient list. Her eyes stop and hover over a patient's name that she is very sure she recognises. Yes, that is right, Chloe Hamson. It couldn't be, could it? Maybe it was just a coincidence. Amy was very surprised to be reading her old school friend's name. She double checked and it said that Chloe had been admitted three weeks ago with a nervous breakdown and she was now into the recovery stages of her treatment and due for discharge the beginning of next week. Amy made her way out onto the wing where the bedrooms were and walked along until she found room 9. Chloe's name was on the name card on the door. Amy hesitated and then knocked gently on the door.

'Come in' came a small voice from inside. Amy knew then it was definitely her old school friend and opened the door.

'Hi Chloe' Amy said. 'How are you?'

'Hi' Chloe said with a look of confusion on her face, she was sat up in bed reading a book. She put the book down and said 'Amy?'

'Yeah it's me' Amy replied. 'I work as a nurse at this hospital and recognised your name on the list.' 'I hope you don't mind me coming in to see you.'

'Oh no not at all, in fact a friendly face is just what I need right now.' Chloe replied.

'So, how come you are in here?' Amy asked and Chloe said 'How long have you got?'

And Amy sat down next to her and said 'Ages, if you want to talk about it?' And so Chloe began her story.

You realise you are grown up when you hit your twenties. Leaving university, getting that first job and moving to a flat with your friends. Your own life in your hands and the whole of your future ahead of you. Dreams about meeting someone special, getting that promotion, a house, a mortgage, maybe even marriage and children are starting to cross your mind. It's an exciting time and Chloe and her friends had dreamt about all these things.

Chloe was always the life and soul of the party, living each week for the weekend and for the Saturday night out with her group of good school friends. It was a high to rush to get ready and gather around one of their flats to drink vodka cocktails and plan the night ahead. It inevitably went along with some out of tune karaoke, blind drunk sway dancing and a trip to the kebab shop on the way home. For as long as she can remember they had done this, throughout sixth form, those were some of the craziest times of her life and it continued well into their university years. Her friends would all travel to someone's university town and get together for a good old night out on the town. Even after university when they had all got jobs in London this just made it even easier to get together and go out, living life in the fast lane.

Many a night Chloe found herself saying, I'll stop drinking at midnight. I don't want to be sick in the morning; I can't have another horrible hangover because they're just way too bad for words. Then, she'd get carried away in the moment and with the offers of a drink from a friend her worries were soon forgotten. Before she knew it she'd had eight vodka red bulls and felt fabulous. Many a night, Chloe and her friends would get through a bottle or two of vodka before they went out and another half a bottle each before the night was out. It's funny because at the time when you're out drinking, spending £30 on shots and vodka red bulls and that kebab, it all seems so worthwhile and yet the next day you just wonder why you feel so rough. Chloe was always sick the next day and suffered for at least 4 or 5 hours just stuck sleeping it all off in bed. This became the normal pattern of her life, go out Saturday and live it up, just to spend all day Sunday stuck to her mattress watching Holly oaks and Friends with puke never far from her lips. Classy but so true.

Chloe had recently been on holiday to Val de Sere Skiing. A seven day holiday involving a lot of partying every night until 4 am in the morning. There had been lots of drinking and a distinct lack of sleep.

Chloe explained to Amy. It all started the day she returned from holiday. It had been a mad week with a girl friend called Clare who she knew from work. The holiday had tired Chloe out and after wards she was visiting her parents for the weekend before returning back to London for work. Her parents lived in Kent and when they picked her up from the airport she slept all the way home in the car. When she got home it was late evening but she was wide awake and wired. Her parents went to bed and Chloe had a shower and noticed that she was feeling really out of sorts. She had really broken sleep and the only way to describe how she felt was delirious. She kept imagining shadows jumping out of the air and everything around her felt surreal. She finally fell asleep the early hours of the morning but was wide awake again at 6am. Chloe felt shaky and dizzy so she drank a glass of water and sat with a bowl next to her in case she was going to be sick. Her parents came down to breakfast and asked her what was wrong. She still felt like everything was in a dream and they all concluded she was just over tired and maybe suffering from slight sleep deprivation. By Sunday night Chloe wasn't feeling any better and felt drained. It was at night time that the shadows started to look like shapes in the air and it was as if her brain was going into over drive. She was wide awake when she felt absolutely shattered.

On Monday morning there was no way Chloe was getting the train up to London to go back to work. So she stayed on the sofa feeling freezing and physically her whole body shook. She managed to get some sleep that day and by the evening was feeling a bit better. Her parents decided she looked better and they agreed she could travel back up to London that evening ready for work the next day. Chloe got back to London at 7.30 pm and her flat mate Rosie was in when she got there.

'Whoa you look rough' she commented as Chloe walked through into the living room.

'Yeah I had a mad week and I've been feeling really ill ever since, straight to bed for me!' Chloe replied.

'Oh ok, hope you feel better in the morning' Rosie said concerned.

A few hours later after a broken sleep Chloe got out of bed and wrapped her dressing gown around herself, she was shaking freezing cold again and she was sick in the toilet bowl. Rosie was still up and brought her some water. Chloe was mumbling something about how her mum had been having an affair. Rosie was a bit taken aback and passed the water to Chloe. 'What do you mean?' Rosie asked sounding confused.

'My mum she has been having an affair with my neighbour' Chloe said blankly.

Rosie noticed Chloe's stare was straight ahead and her eyes were glazed over. They were transfixed on one point and she started to cry. Rosie helped Chloe up from the floor near the toilet and helped her into the living room and onto the sofa.

'I'm sure that's not true, why do you think this?' Rosie asked trying to make sense of this random accusation.

'I just do, it's obvious.' Chloe replied between sobs. The tears rolled uncontrollably from her eyes. She sat there for half an hour motionless just staring straight ahead. Repeating the same thing about an affair and generally not making much sense.

Rosie was worried but didn't really know what to do. She sat there and listened and put a blanket around Chloe. She turned the TV on to try and provide a distraction for Chloe, it worked, she stopped crying and turned her head to watch repeats of Eastenders and Coronation Street that were on Sky Plus. They both fell asleep in the living room at around midnight.

About 2 am, Chloe found herself wide awake again and she was seeing the shadows in the air, one of the shadows was like a snake's mouth open and coming straight for her face. It was so real and made Chloe feel like her breathing was shallow and she started to panic. She got up and went out to the toilet, shaking she was sick again and didn't know what to do with herself. She put her hand up in front of herself as if to stop the images of the snake getting to her. Chloe thought this must be what it is like when some one is tripping out on drugs, not that she'd ever taken a drug in her life and so actually wouldn't have a clue what it was like.

She couldn't sleep for the rest of the night and found the only distraction from the images was to pick up and read an Argos catalogue; it was the only book in the room. After what felt like hours morning came round and she tried to have a shower. She couldn't handle the sensation of the water on her skin and felt claustrophobic. Chloe had never felt like this before, it was scary and she felt like she was having an out of body experience. Rosie saw Chloe come out of the bathroom shaking in her towel. 'Are you ok?' Rosie asked.

'I don't know' Chloe replied almost child like. Rosie was really worried, she told Chloe not to go to work and that she would take her to the doctors. They got dressed, Chloe put on mismatched clothes and Rosie decided not to say anything. They got the overland train from where they lived to the doctors, one stop up. Chloe was constantly shaking, crying and staring into nowhere. Rosie guided her up the steps and spoke to the receptionist for her. The receptionist alerted a doctor and she was taken straight through. Rosie should have gone in with her but Chloe had insisted she go in on her own. The doctor saw Chloe who continually cried and seemed confused. Chloe could see the doctor's mouth moving but could not really hear or understand what he was saying. A prescription was handed to her and she was sent back out to reception, told not to go to work for the rest of the week and to take the anti depressants he had prescribed her.

Rosie took her to the pharmacy to get the prescription and then they went home. Chloe took the tablets and Rosie saw that she got a blanket over her on the sofa. Rosie apologised 'I have to go into work now, will you be alright?' She asked. 'Yeah, I'm ok now' Chloe replied. And so Rosie went off to work.
Chloe was still experiencing the shadow shapes in front of her vision but she hadn't told the doctor or Rosie. Still everything felt like it was floating. She hoped the tablets would make her feel better.
An hour later things were getting worse and Chloe was hallucinating. She had been dozing on the sofa and when she woke up she had the craziest thought that the air freshener on the table next to her was an oxygen machine pumping oxygen into the room to keep her alive. She sat transfixed on the air freshener watching it pump out every 15 minutes. Time must have gone by and soon Rosie was home and she saw Chloe just staring into nowhere again. Rosie thought it was as if Chloe was only half there. Rosie didn't know what to do, it was so scary seeing your friend like a complete stranger, mumbling nonsense and obviously not very well. She knew the doctor had given her anti depressants and Rosie just didn't know what else to do. She decided if Chloe was still like this tomorrow she would get her to go back to the doctor, something really wasn't right. They watched TV and Chloe was crying to herself. Rosie listened when Chloe talked and put a blanket over her when she finally fell asleep.

The next day Chloe had a shower and although she was still shaking and looked drained, she was more coherent and put some washing on. Rosie decided Chloe would be alright for the day and had to go into work. At 11am Chloe suddenly decided to go out of the flat and get some milk and bread because they didn't have any left. The strange thing was before she left she had just eaten some toast and there was nearly a full loaf of bread on the side. On the table was an open book of Banksy Art work and Chloe had been staring at the same page for an hour. She went out of the house with only a handful of change and her door key, nothing else.
She walked down the path to the road and immediately felt like she was in a dream and floating along. She turned down the road towards the shop and a man walked by, she felt really self conscious like the man was staring at her. She kept on walking at a fast military pace with her arms waving and must have looked quite ridiculous to passers by. She felt really ill but kept walking, everything flashed by in a blur and then as she came to the roundabout across from the shop she saw a sign for the police station. For some strange reason she knew she had to go there, and changed course. She hurried along the road, thinking that every car that passed her was staring at her. Then she finally got to the police station and without a moments thought she walked straight in, placed her cash

and keys on the front desk and said 'I need to talk to someone'. The policeman looked a bit shocked and very concerned. He told her to take a seat and someone would be out in a minute. Chloe sat on the edge of the seat and her legs shook. She looked very shifty and something was definitely wrong with her the policeman thought. He radioed for a female police officer to come out and talk to her, Chloe was taken into a secure room just off from the reception area and asked what was wrong. Chloe just broke down crying, mumbling about how her mum had had an affair and always told her to cut labels out of her clothes. She was making no sense, putting her hand up in front of her face and her breathing was very shallow, taking short sharp breathes with her chest rising and falling very fast. The police lady realised that this was a case for the hospital and not a criminal matter. They asked her for her address and tried to calm Chloe down. After a while they drove her up to the nearest hospital and Chloe sat in the back of the car trying hard to breath. It was as if she was having a really bad panic attack.

When they got to the hospital Chloe didn't really understand where she was but she felt relieved that she was at a hospital and that was good because she felt really ill. It was only then she realised that they were in the mental health ward of the hospital and she had been put in an observation room with 2 nurses. They told her she would have to stay in the hospital for observation and would she like a glass of water. Chloe accepted the water but immediately started to think it had been poisoned with a drug by the doctors. She was extremely paranoid and still making very little sense. Rosie had been called because that was the only person Chloe had said for her next of kin. Rosie turned up later with a bag of clothes and things for Chloe. Chloe had been assessed by two psychologists who were concerned about her delusions and paranoia. She was admitted to the ward and put under the mental health act, sectioned for her own safety so she couldn't leave the ward.

When Chloe first entered the ward a nurse took her down a long grey corridor. Chloe had never been to hospital before, and certainly didn't think she'd get to see the inside of her local mental health ward of her hospital that was for sure. The main communal living room was filled with plastic covered hospital chairs and all the other patients were staring at her. Chloe was told to take a seat and wait for her room to be prepared. She suddenly realised the gravity of the situation and tears started to roll down her face. She had no idea why she was here and she felt very scared. A girl, one of the other patients saw that Chloe was crying and tried to cheer her up by offering her a cookie. Chloe accepted it out of politeness. Then a nurse came out and took her to her room. The room consisted of a small thin single bed with a sheet and a blue hospital blanket. A basin and a cupboard. The room was bare and Chloe felt lonely. The nurse put her bags on the floor near the cupboard and left Chloe to settle in.

Chloe just curled up on the bed feeling disorientated, confused and tearful. She continued to cry for the next three days, visits from doctors and nurses were all a blur and then they put her on medication to stabilise her mood and help her with the confusion and paranoia. They moved her to a ward with only curtains for privacy and she had to share with 5 other women. One girl next to her was playing really loud drum and bass music all day long and this was really annoying. Chloe felt so lost, why was she here, why did she keep hallucinating and seeing all of these weird shadows in her vision. She soon found that the medication she had been given had a sedative effect and her escape from it all was to sleep. Nurses kept coming in to check on her every hour and she would drift in and out of sleep. Was she crazy? What was happening to her, she felt so scared and alone.

Eventually Chloe's parents had been called and they came straight to visit her. Chloe was very unresponsive but knew her parents were there and her mum gave her a really long hug. Chloe seemed like she was somewhere else in her thoughts and this was very upsetting for her parents to see their daughter this way. They had been told by the doctors that she was experiencing a mental breakdown and part of this would include paranoia, confusion, anxiety and tearfulness.

A week past by and the medication started to work, Chloe became more responsive and started to talk to the nurses and she had counselling sessions to try and make sense of what had happened to her. She was told that they thought her breakdown had been caused by sleep deprivation and drinking too much alcohol. Hopefully now that she was sleeping regularly and taking the medication she should make a full recovery. She would be kept in the hospital for two more weeks to be observed and then she would be allowed to go home.

'Wow, that sounds like a horrible ordeal Chloe' said Amy who had been listening intently to Chloe for the last hour. 'I'm so glad you are alright now.'
'So am I' smiled Chloe.
'Anyway that's plenty about me, how are you?' Chloe asked.
'Oh I'm fine' replied Amy.
'That's good, do you realise we haven't spoken for about 4 years. The last time I saw you was at a party in London when you were still with Shane. What happened to you and Shane? I heard you split up?' Chloe asked.
'Yeah we did.' Replied Amy.
'Why did you leave the city so suddenly I thought you had a job at Kings College hospital all lined up?' Chloe said.
Amy sighed this was a long story but she was so tired of holding back and after all this time she decided to finally let it all out and started to tell Chloe everything. It was only the second person she had ever told.

It had all begun in her first year at medical school. Amy had studied at King's College University to become a nurse and this is where she had met junior trainee doctor Shane Edwards. They met on the first day of term at the union. Amy had been wandering around aimlessly looking for the job shop and getting herself very lost in the big building with seemingly endless corridors. She went to turn the corner and walked straight into a somewhat handsome tall guy. He held out a hand in front of him and steadied her as she was starting to fall. She looked up into his deep brown eyes and their gazes met.
'Oh sorry' Amy stuttered as she wobbled on her feet.
'No worries' replied Shane as he held her hand to steady her. 'Are you ok?' He asked.
They continued to chat and Shane invited her out for a drink that evening. They soon became an item and dated for 3 years solidly throughout university. It was a text

book romance, where they could barely spend a moment alone and had to be with each other every spare minute of the day. In the third year they shared a room together in a house with some friends, it just made sense because they spent every night together and it would save them on rent. They went to the movies, went ice skating and even met each others' parents. It was the stuff dreams were made of and Amy was blissfully happy and in love.

However some dreams are not built to last and it all went wrong in their third and final year. Amy had just left her last lecture of the day and she sent Shane a quick text asking him what he would like for dinner?

He didn't reply which was very unlike him. She stopped off at the shop to pick up some chicken and rice for her curry recipe she planned to cook Shane tonight.

It is a horrible winter night and they live about 10 minutes away from the shop. Amy battled along the road to their house in the pouring rain dragging her shopping bag and umbrella along with her. As she rounds the corner she can see a light is on in their room at the front of the house and she thinks to herself how strange it is that Shane didn't text her back. She puts the key in the door and calls out 'Hi Shane'. There is no response. Amy wanders into the kitchen and puts the shopping on the side. No one else is in and she wonders where everyone is at this time of night. She can hear muffled voices upstairs and thinks it must be Shane and one of their housemates. She climbs the stairs and goes to push the door open to their room and greet them. She stands in the door entrance in what can only be described as a state of pure shock. There in front of her, in her bed, is a girl half clothed trying desperately to pull her top over her bony half naked body. The girl is very tanned and petite, the complete opposite to Amy, with long black shiny hair and a face covered in thick make up. Shane is walking towards her with a look of guilt and remorse plastered across his face.

'Babe, I'm so sorry.' Shane says weakly, knowing there is no way he is going to get out of this one. 'Amy just shakes her head in disbelief as hot tears stream down her cheeks full of anger and hurt. She turns and walks back down the landing and locks herself in the bathroom. She collapse in a heap on the floor and sobs her heart out. She can hear the girl talking to Shane and then shortly after the front door shuts and Amy can hear Shane coming back up the stairs.

'Amy', please, come out; we need to talk about this…' He pleads.

'No.' Is all Amy can manage. Her heart is breaking and she can't see in front of here as the tears blur her vision. She stays in the bathroom for a least an hour and when she finally musters the courage to come out Shane is no where to be seen. She takes her chance, grabs her gym bag and heads out of the house. She calls her friend Emma and asks if she can come round later and stay the night. There is no way she is going back to Shane.

'Whoa, I had no idea.' Chloe says once Amy has finished her story about how Shane and her had split up and how Amy had never been out with another man since.

'Yeah, it was pretty bad, he hurt me beyond belief' Amy said. 'Anyway, we've been chatting for hours and I'd better get on and do some work. It was lovely to see you and I'm so glad you are ok now and will be getting out of here soon. Take care of yourself and we should meet up soon.' Amy offered.

'Yes that would be nice; I am staying with my parents for a few weeks so we should definitely catch up. Chloe replied.

That evening after her eventful day filling in at the psychiatric ward, Amy was back in her home, the evening had crept in and Amy watched as the last of the daylight drew away outside the window. She had certainly been an agony aunt today. First Chloe and now Matt. Matt had come round a few hours ago and Amy had finally got up off the sofa to go to bed properly about 3 am; Matt is asleep sat upright in the armchair opposite her. He hadn't wanted to be on his own and had eventually drifted of after talking for what had been hours. Poor Matt he was so worried about his sick brother. Michael was back in hospital - still with no match for a donor. Amy wished there was something she could do except listen.

She also felt a sense of relief that she had taken Chloe's advice and finally told Matt about Shane. He now understood why she was so distant if he asked about her university years and why she never went out on dates. It felt like she had no secrets left to keep from Matt and it felt good for the truth to be out. As he slept Amy couldn't help but notice in the dim twilight that he didn't half seem attractive. She sighed, why after all these years was he still single, such a catch and yet not so much as a date or two that he had ever told her about. She leaned over and replaced the blanket onto his shoulders and finally took herself off to bed.

Chapter 21

Sue

Face book status – Fingers crossed…

Sue is really worried about her son. It is 2 weeks after Christmas and Michael is still in hospital because of his Liver failure. He is very ill, tired, weak and sick. There is a small chance that he could get a donor and so they are keeping him in hospital ready for when they can do the operation. Matt is at his brothers's bedside and Amy pops her head around the door.

'Hi boys, how are you doing?' Amy asks as she enters the room with a big bunch of flowers.

'What are you doing here?' Matt asks in surprise and a smile breaks on his worry torn face.

'I've just finished my shift for the day and thought I'd come down to see how your brother is doing? Plus I've brought these flowers, not very masculine but I thought they'd brighten up the room.' Amy says. 'How are you Michael?' Amy asks.

'Oh I'm bearing up ok thanks Amy. Just waiting in hope really.' Michael replies. He looks really weak and helpless for a grown man. Amy smiles and puts the flowers down on the side. 'Well hopefully it will be good news for you soon' Amy says.

As if by divine intervention, the doctor knocks on the door and asks if he can have a moment alone with Michael and Matt. Amy leaves the room and sits outside on a hard plastic chair wondering what it could be about and whether she dare consider it could be the good news they had all been waiting for. The door flies open and Matt runs out to greet Amy 'They've found a donor' He almost shouts. Everyone in the corridor turns round to see what the commotion is and Amy jumps up and gives Matt a big hug.

'Wow, that is amazing, I'm so happy for you all' Amy replies. Matt has a beaming smile on his face and they go back in to the room and Michael already looks better sat up in bed with a matching smile across his face.

Matt's mum is called and soon they are all at his bedside with celebratory cups of tea and coffee from the vending machine. The operation has been scheduled for later that day and Amy decides it is best to leave the family to it. Amy gives her best wishes for the operation and says she will visit again in a few days.

A few days later and the operation has gone successfully. Amy visits Michael with Matt and Michael tells Matt he wants to have a party to celebrate his near death escape. It is Matt's responsibility to organise the party for a week on Saturday the day Michael is released from hospital. Amy offers to help with the arrangements and they start to make a list of guests.

While they are sat at Matt's house making a list for the party Amy thinks it might be time to tell Matt that she is going to Haiti to volunteer and that she is leaving next Monday. Matt is shocked and impressed all at the same time. He thinks it is such a brave thing to do and tells Amy that he is very proud of her. He also looks a little forlorn and Amy reassures him it is only two months and that he won't have time to miss her.

Chapter 22

Matt

Face book status – Party time!

Amy is all packed for her trip to Haiti and now it is party time. It is Saturday morning and Amy has just got to Matt's house laden with balloons and tablecloths and everything they need for the party. The party is being held down the road in the local community hall. Matt loads up the car with all of the supplies and they head there to set everything up. The building is a lovely old wooden building white washed and bright. There are windows covering all of the walls of the main room and there is a great view across the local playing field with tall trees lining the edge. It is a lovely January morning and the sun is streaming through the trees.

What a wonderful place to have a party Amy thinks to herself as she lays the table cloths out onto the long tables they have around the edges for the buffet food. Amy and Matt work hard pumping up helium balloons and putting up welcome home banners in every corner. They are done by 2pm and head home to grab a short rest and showers before they have to be back tonight at 6pm to set up the food. Michaels mum Sue is busy preparing all the food and has enlisted Sally to help. It is a joint effort with everyone pitching in; even Lily and Ben are helping decorate the fairy cakes with icing.

6pm

Amy has just arrived back at the community hall and is getting out of her car cautiously in her high heels. She has chosen to wear her hair down, a rare occasion for her and she is wearing a flattering black dress that has three layers to the skirt. She looks beautiful and Zoe has already complimented her as they got ready together. Zoe is halfway across the car park and almost into the hall by the time Amy has managed to get out of the car and lock it up. Matt's car rolls down the entrance to the car park and he sees a gorgeous girl walking unsteadily in high heels across the car park. He can't believe his eyes when he realises it is Amy. He hasn't ever seen her dressed up like this before and cannot take his eyes off her. His heart starts to beat faster and he has butterflies. He carefully parks the car alongside Amy's and gets out.

'Hi Amy' he mutters, not sure what else to say.
'Hey Matt' Amy replies and turns back to look his way. 'Looking lovely' Matt decides to say as he walks towards her. 'Thanks, you look good in a suit' Amy replies and giggles nervously. They hug and then turn away quickly to walk inside. 'So, is everything set for tonight?' Amy asks. 'Yes, mum is already inside setting up the food for the buffet. So I think we are almost ready to go.' Matt says. They walk into the room and the DJ is playing with the microphone testing his equipment. There are fairy lights all over the ceiling beams and the place looks magical. 'Good job' Amy says and Matt turns and smiles at her. It isn't long before the first guests will arrive and both Matt and Amy take the chance to go to the now empty bar and grab a glass of wine each.

Amy's phone starts to ring and it is Chloe. Amy invited Chloe to the party as they had been out for a drink last week and Amy thought it would be nice to invite her along. 'Hi Chloe' Amy answered the call. 'Hi Amy, I'm a bit lost do I turn right or left at the top of the hill?' Chloe asks anxiously. 'It's the first left once you've gone over the top of the hill' Amy describes. And then they ring off. Amy notices Matt has left her side and is greeting the first of the guests, the party boy Michael has arrived holding hands with Emma. Emma has a beaming smile on her face so happy that Michael has made a full recovery. And just behind them are Ollie and Alex.

Soon the room is full of music and laughter and the party is off to a good start. Amy's parents are here and so are Amy's cousins, Ben and Lily. They have been allowed to invite a friend each and are currently dancing in the bubbles and dry ice smoke that the DJ is making on the dance floor. Amy walks over to Chloe who has been introduced to Zoe and they are deep in conversation.
'Oh Hi Amy, I wondered where you had gone?' Zoe asks with a cheeky look on her face. Amy wonders what they had been talking about before she had walked over to them. Chloe breaks the silence and compliments Amy on a great party. 'So, I was wondering...' Chloe said. 'Who is that guy over there at the bar with Matt?' Chloe is looking over at the bar and hinting which one she means.
'The guy with the dark blue shirt?' Amy asks. 'Yes!' Chloe replies. 'Oh he is Alex. He is a friend of a friend to Matt; I think he knows him from football. He is an architect.' Amy describes. 'Why, do you like him?' Amy teases and both her and Zoe laugh. Chloe goes red and just says 'Maybe'.
'I'll introduce you if you'd like?' Amy offers and off they trot in the direction of the bar. Zoe turns to the buffet table and decides to make herself busy with some food. Sue and Michael are talking with Ted and Sally and complimenting her for such wonderful food.

There is a U2 song playing in the back ground 'With or without you' and everyone is having a wonderful time. Chloe is now deep in conversation with Alex and Ollie has found Zoe at the buffet table. This leaves Matt and Amy alone at the bar and just on cue a slow song by Norah Jones comes on and soon there are several couples taking to the dance floor. Matt looks over at Amy with a nervous smile and decides it is about time he got some courage. He puts his hand out in front of Amy and says 'Care to dance Miss Lucas?'
Amy smiles and decides it would only be polite to accept his offer. They walk hand in hand to the dance floor and tentatively move closer to one another. The song plays on and they sway in time to the music. Amy tries to think of something appropriate to say and just as she opens her mouth to speak Matt surprises her and leans down and places his lips softly on hers. It is like magic, her lips tingle with the sensation and she can't believe she is actually kissing Matt. The moment only lasts a few seconds but it is longer than a lifetime to her. They pull away to the sound of applause coming from their parents and Zoe who all give them knowing looks as if they knew it would happen. Matt smiles shyly and looks back down at Amy. 'How embarrassing' he says. Amy looks up into his eyes and just laughs. Matt stutters and then decides to be brave and says 'I love you Amy'. Amy's smile grows and she has tears in her eyes 'I love you too.' She is blissfully

happy nothing could spoil this moment. Then she realises that she is going to Haiti in two days time. 'I'm going to miss you loads.' Matt replies as if reading her mind. 'But I know you have got to go and hold some hands and I'll be here waiting for you when you get back.'

Meanwhile, Michael and Emma are leaving in a taxi because Michael is obviously still recovering from the liver transplant and needs his rest. On the way home Michael turns to Emma and out of his pocket he produces a ring. He proposes to Emma and simply says 'Marry me'. Emma kisses Michael.

The next day Chloe and Alex go on their first date. They decide to go to the cinema and watch a repeat of the film Love actually. They arrange to go to the cinema every week and it becomes a regular occurrence.

Zoe and Ollie exchanged numbers at the party but they never saw each other again.
Tom and Lily see each other every day of the holidays and Lily is very happy.

Chapter 23

Matt

Face book status – is so happy that Amy is back home!

Amy has recently returned from saving lives. She thought her parents were going to collect her from the airport. Unbeknown to her and Matt had arranged a surprise and he is currently waiting at the airport nervously with a bunch of flowers. Amy is dragging her suitcase behind her and looks out across the crowd of people to try and see her parents. They aren't anywhere to be seen and then she sees matt standing there smiling at her with a bunch of beautiful flowers and she runs to him, drops her suitcase on the floor and wraps her arms around him. They hug for an eternity and then he says 'let's get you home Ames.' As they are sat in the car on the drive home Amy tells him about the devastation she witnessed and he listens attentively.

They go back to Matt's house and he puts the kettle on and they have a nice cup of tea. He puts the flowers in some water for Amy and then he turns to Amy and asks her if she would like to stay the night rather than go home. They have some supper and Amy falls asleep on the sofa after the long flight, she must have jet lag Matt thinks and puts a blanket over her. He turns the light off and goes to bed.

The next morning, Matt wakes up early and makes breakfast for Amy. Amy is surprised as he brings her toast and tea. This is lovely she thinks and says 'I could get used to this Matt' and smiles a cheeky grin.

It's Sunday night and Amy has to go back to her parent's house as she has work early the next morning. She goes home with a heavy heart; she misses Matt already and consoles herself that she'll see him tonight.

7.30pm

Amy has just finished work and she is so excited to see Matt again. She arrives at his house and there is a lovely smell of cooking. He has cooked a lovely curry and there are candles lit on the table. It is so romantic. They eat and talk and watch a movie. Then he drives her home.

11pm

Amy's parents are planning a holiday to New Zealand. They have bought a travel guide and are planning to visit some friends who live out there. They are flying to Auckland and then they are going to hire a car and drive around the North and the South Island sightseeing.

They plan to go to visit Mount Cook, near a beautiful area where there are mountains surrounding a lake called Lake Tekapo. There is a Glacier and a great walk to take through the glacial valley.

Amy listened to there plans and is happy for them to be going on such a wonderful holiday.

Chapter 24

Face book status: we are off to New Zealand

February 2011

Amy's parents have just got to Heathrow Terminal 4. They have booked the trip for 6 weeks and are so happy for the break. They check in at the airport and are given free upgrades to First Class. They wait in the airport for what seems like an eternity. Once aboard the flight they take their seats and Amy's mum is a very nervous flyer. She suffers from vertigo and travel sickness. She takes her pills and settles down to read her book. Amy's dad has a whisky to calm his nerves. The plane takes off and the air stewardess hands out tea and coffee and lunch. The flight takes approximately 12 hours to Hong Kong where there is a stopover and then another 10 hours to reach New Zealand.

They land safely at Auckland airport and it is sunny with blue skies it is the summer season in New Zealand and the weather is glorious. They step off the plane and onto a bus where they are transported to the terminal for passport control and baggage reclaim. Once all cleared, they step outside of the airport and hail a taxi to take them to their hotel in Auckland. They are severely jet lagged and sleep it off for about 4 hours. It is evening when they wake up and they decide to go out for dinner.

They wander through the streets of this modern city hand in hand and find a lovely Italian restaurant to eat at. They share a bottle of wine, eat pasta dishes and finish off with ice cream for dessert. Then they retire to the hotel as they are still jet lagged.

The next morning the hotel concierge have arranged for the hire car to be delivered to the hotel for Amy's parents. They pack up their suitcases and get the lift down to the reception area where the lovely silver car is parked. They set off to see their friends who live near the bay of plenty. They arrive there just before sundown and their long lost friends greet them with a hug and welcome them into their home. It is a lovely house with photos of family everywhere and flowers in vases and fresh bread cooking in the oven. They catch up on each others lives as they haven't spoken properly for years and have only ever conversed by email. It is a lovely evening and the red wine is flowing.

The following day they pack up the car and head off to the Far North. They arrive at what is described as a wonder of the eyes. It is a beach called Te Werahi Beach it is the most beautiful coast line Amy's parents have ever seen. They visit the 800 year old Pohutukawa tree this is a sacred site and they stare at it in awe. That is a really lovely tree Amy's Mum thinks to herself. Then they drive to the giant sand dunes and toboggan down them as this they were children again. Amy's parents are falling in love all over again. They stay at Pukenui Lodge Motel and rise early for a new day of adventures.

It is the second week of their journey and they drive to the town of Rotorua where there is a Polynesian spa powered by the natural thermal energy of the ground. Her parents laze about in the pools for an hour and enjoy their time together. Their next destination is

Wellington where they stay at the Hilton and live a life of luxury for the night. They visit the Te Papa museum and learn about symbolism, the Maori culture and join in with the Haka. The Maori are the indigenous people of New Zealand. The Haka is a traditional dance. New Zealand is home to the All Blacks rugby team and this year New Zealand is the ambassador for the Rugby World Cup.

After this, they head off to the ferry across to the south island of New Zealand. They visit the Abel Tasman National park and go kayaking. It is so beautiful the sea is crystal blue and the sun is shining on them. They have a tour of the wine region on mountain bikes and try all the flavours of wine on offer.

From here they travel to Mount Cook and discover the church of the good shepherd. The sunlight gleams through the window and the colours of the rainbow reflect through the glass and light up the room. The room is alive with the glory of nature and Amy's parents turn to each other and remember the day the married each other and kiss each other with the love they have for one another.

They stay at a Youth Hostel for the night and then the next morning they travel south to visit Oamaru to see the penguins wadding out of the sea with food for their children.

Then they drive to visit the doubtful sound this is where the river meets the sea, there are waterfalls with rainbows and they spot seals and whales.

Then they visit the Punakaiki Pancake rocks and these are a sight to behold. They have arrived and there is a storm and the clouds go dark and there is energy about them. The waves roll through the cracks in the rocks and water blows out through the blow holes. It is a magnificent display of nature and it makes everyone feel alive and at one with nature.

Before they head home from their travels they buy all of their family presents from a lovely shop in Christ Church.

The six weeks are up and Amy's parents have had a lovely holiday and they'll remember everyone they met and they have a new found love for New Zealand. They have even thought about retiring to this great country.

Chapter 25

Amy

Meanwhile, Amy is home without her parents, as they have gone on holiday to New Zealand. She invites her friend Zoe to stay with her and has the best time. She talks with Zoe about their relationships and they laugh and joke with one another about their other halves.

'Zoe, how is Isaac then?' Amy asks.
'He's great thanks Amy; he is the love of my life!' Zoe is beaming with joy.
'We went to the cinema the other night and watched a rom com it was so romantic. We had a meal first and then watched the film.
'Oooh sounds a lot like love to me... you love him; you want to marry him...' Amy teases.
All Zoe can do is smile bashfully.
'How is Matt?' Zoe changes the subject swiftly.
'Yeah he's good thanks Zoe. He loves his job, he works so hard and I am really proud of him. He is such a kind man and he has a good heart.' Amy says proudly.

Matt stays with Amy most nights at her house and they go out swimming and walking and to the pub. Matt and Amy have fallen in love.

One night they play scrabble and it is so funny because they make up words that don't exist and generally just make each other laugh. Matt suddenly turns to Amy and asks if she would live with him. Amy's nearly cries and then just smiles outwardly with joy and happiness. Matt holds her close and promises he'll never let her go.
'I love you Amy' Matt says.
'I love you Matt' Amy says.

Later that evening, they have a very serious conversation about love and families and how important it is to put your family first. They talk about God and how they were religious when they were younger yet somewhere along the way they lost their faith. They laugh at how serious the conversation has turned and then they kiss. Amy is the happiest woman in the world right now and cannot wait to tell her parents the good news.

Chapter 26

Lily

Lily has recovered from the vodka incident and is at school. Her favourite subject is Art and she loves to paint with water colours. Her teacher is a calm and lovely lady. She encourages Lily and today she is painting a rose. It is white and she paints the stem brown. She loves art and when she is a grown up she wants to be an artist. Both her grandma and her granny are artists and she admires them. She hopes to be as good as them one day. Both her grandma and granny are kind and gentle women with a hearts of gold. They cook her lovely food when she stays with them.

It is Friday night. Lily is staying with her grandma tonight and she loves staying overnight there. Her gran has every art material under the sun and teachers her how to create artwork with pastels, oil and how to sketch with pencils. Today they are painting Brock hill park, a lovely nature park. There are silver birch trees and the sun is breaking though the clouds. Lily sketches the outline of the trees and then with water colour she develops the piece of artwork and about three hours later it is complete.

It is winter outside and the snow is falling on the ground. Her grandma says she can make a snowman tomorrow. They cook supper together and her grandma has baked a lovely fruitcake for pudding. Her grandpa arrives home from work and they all sit at the table at eat the food. Then her grandpa clears away the table and washes up. Lily loves her grandparents they are so considerate and share the workload around the house. It must be true love and she smiles to herself.

The next morning, Lily and her grandpa go outside and make a snowman. The snow has fallen everywhere and it is a beautiful sight. They roll the snow and make a body and a head. The choose sprouts from the garden for eyes and a twig so the snowman has a smile. They give the snowman arms made of twigs as well. Lily laughs with happiness and they take a photo so she can remember this special day she has shared with her grandpa.

The following day is Sunday and they go to church. It is a lovely church called St Leonard's and it is where Lily's mum and dad were married. Her grandma holds her hand and they stroll through the snow until they arrive at the marvelous building. The architecture is amazing and Lily loves it here because it is a sanctuary. They join the rest of the community and sing the hymns. They listen to the priest who reads extracts from the bible. Then they say the Lord's Prayer. As they walk out of the church everyone greets each other and wishes each other a good day.

Chapter 27

April 2011

Amy's parents have returned from their holiday and they are full of happiness and a new found love for everyone. They excitably give Amy her present a handmade piece of wood carved in the shape of a heart. Amy thanks them and gives them both a hug. They hug Matt and Amy cannot wait any more.

'I have the greatest news mum and dad.' Amy says.
'Yes......' her dad says.
'Matt has asked me to live with him and I have said yes!' Amy beams with joy.
'Oh wow, love that is such great news.' Her mum hugs her.

'Excellent news Matt' Amy's dad shakes his hand. 'Good man'.

They have a celebratory meal. Amy's mum and dad cook a roast dinner with all the trimmings. They have roast beef, Yorkshire puddings, horseradish sauce, roast potatoes, vegetables and gravy. It is delicious. Just what you need for a Sunday when the weather is still quite cold and spring is not quite here yet.

After they have finished the food they all clear up together and then relax and put on some music and talk about their travels. There are at least 1000 photos to be seen and Amy rolls her eyes at Matt who has to stifle a giggle and listen intently to Amy's parents.

Later that year Amy and Matt move into a small house with two bedrooms. They hire a removal van and pack their belongings from their parents' houses into it. There is an argument between Amy and Amy's mum over who bought the TV for the spare room and Matt just reassures Amy that they can buy a new one. Amy's mum feels immediately guilty and offers them to have it and all is forgiven. Amy and Matt love their new house. They decorate it all with green and white and brown, their other family members all contribute furniture and there are family photos everywhere.

Everyone is welcomed into their home with open arms. Amy has Zoe and Isaac over to eat with them. Matt asks Ollie and his partner over to eat. Lily and Ben, Amy's cousins stay over for a sleep over. Michael and Emma have a new born baby now and they visit often. Amy has always had one philosophy that she maintains throughout her life, that if all you can do for anyone is give them food, hold their hand and listen to them, then that is a good way to live your life.

This is a true love story. It is about goodness, hope and adversity against all odds.

There are a boy and a girl who meet by chance at a party.

They date and enjoy life together; they witness tragedy, death and life's miracles.

Above all it is a story about family and the love they have for you.

Hi everyone,

Firstly, I really hope you enjoy the book!

And secondly, about me...... I currently work in a call centre and I have a love for the South East of Kent. I was born in Britain, the hometown of Ashford and I am very proud of where I come from. I went to the Folkestone School for girls then I went to university and studied Marketing and Management at the University of Newcastle upon Tyne. I have a love for writing and this is my first novel.

Sarah x

Zeitfracht Medien GmbH
Ferdinand-Jühlke-Straße 7
99095 Erfurt, Deutschland
produktsicherheit@kolibri360.de

Druck:
CPI Druckdienstleistungen GmbH
im Auftrag der
Zeitfracht Medien GmbH
Ein Unternehmen der Zeitfracht - Gruppe
Ferdinand-Jühlke-Str. 7
99095 Erfurt